GIRL FUN 1

Adventures in Lesbian loving

A collection of twenty erotic stories

Edited by Miranda Forbes

Published by Accent Press Ltd – 2009
ISBN 9781906373672

Printed and bound in the UK

Cover Design by
Red Dot Design

Contents

Toy Story
by Lynn Lake

"Wanna hang out at my place after work?" Talia asked.

"Uh, yeah, sure, whatever," I replied, handing a cute guy his change. He smiled at me, sort of stroked my fingers as I dumped the coins into his hand.

Talia rolled her eyes and shouted, "Next!"

I'd been working at the gas station-restaurant for about a month, and despite our obvious differences, Talia and I had really hit it off. She's a funky sort of goth/punk girl, skinny, with long, straight black hair and real pale skin. She has a stud in her nose and a broken heart tattoo on her left shoulder. And her dark eyes are rimmed with enough liner to make Ashlee Simpson jealous. I'm a bit of a girly-girl, myself, petite, with shoulder-length blonde hair, green eyes, and what my mom calls 'an utterly adorable smile'.

Talia normally worked the front cash register and pumped gas, while I waitressed in the restaurant. I was earning extra spending money for college in the fall. Talia was working fulltime to support herself.

"What's the address again?" I asked, when we'd hopped in my car at quitting time. The gas station was way on the outskirts of town. Talia normally took the bus to and from work.

"Just drive, Daisy," she said. "I'll steer you in the right direction."

I giggled. My dad would've had a fit if he'd seen me hanging around with a girl like Talia. I started the car up and Talia punched on the radio. Hillary Duff came tinkling over the loudspeakers.

Talia stuck a finger in her throat and pretended to barf. "You listen to this shit?"

I blushed, checked both ways for traffic before pulling out onto the highway. "Uh ... sometimes," I mumbled, as Talia laughed.

She fiddled around with the radio until she got a heavy metal station, then amped it up so loud I thought my head would explode. It didn't, and half-an-hour later I pulled up in front of a row of townhouses in a kind of crummy area of town. "Looks nice," I said.

"Looks like shit," Talia said. She pointed a purple-tipped finger at the last townhouse in line. "I live in number six."

I glanced around, at the rusty cars lining the street, the group of skuzzy guys hanging around outside the convenience store on the corner. "Um, maybe I better be gettin' home, Talia. I have to –"

"C'mon," she interrupted, turning off the car and pulling out the key. "Don't go chicken-shit on me. There's some stuff I wanna show you."

I followed her into the house. It wasn't too bad, I guess, but it was awfully small. "Are your parents at work?" I asked.

Talia tossed me my car keys, slammed and bolted the door shut. "I just live with my mom. She's at work, yeah. She's got the night shift at the hospital. Wanna beer?"

I shook my head, and Talia grinned. Then she grabbed my hand and pulled me into a bedroom. "There's some stuff I wanna show you," she said again.

I sat on the edge of the bed while she pulled a box out from underneath it – a box full of magazines. She threw one at me. "Take a look at that shit," she said.

I caught the magazine and stared at the glossy front cover. There were two naked women on the cover, a blonde and a brunette; their tongues were touching and their big boobs were pressed together. The magazine was called Lesbian Lickers.

"Uh … huh," I said, feeling kind of scared. I put the magazine down next to me.

"Weird, huh?" Talia said, plopping onto the bed and picking up the dirty magazine. "Think maybe my mom has gone lezzy or somethin'? She hasn't had a date with a guy since Dad dumped her, like, two years ago."

Talia scooched closer, and her leg touched my leg. We were still both in our uniforms – mine a tan blouse and skirt, Talia's a blouse and pair of jeans. She flipped the magazine open. The dark-haired woman was licking and sucking and biting the blonde's big, pink nipples in a series of pictures on one page, sticking her tongue right in the woman's spread-open pink cunny on the next page. My face got all red and my hands damp.

"Crazy, huh?" Talia said. "And take a look at this."

She dropped the open magazine in my lap and clicked on the TV that stood in a corner of the room, the DVD player on top of it. The screen filled up with a naked blonde and brunette. Yup, the same two from the magazine. The blonde was sprawled out on her back on a bed, the brunette working a pink dildo in and out of her cunny.

"My mom's gotta be a lez, huh, Daisy?" Talia said.

I swallowed real hard, my eyes shifting back and forth between the magazine and the TV. I hadn't seen so much

3

porno since Mom and I spring-cleaned my older brother's room one time. "Um, I-I don't know," I mumbled. "Maybe your mother is just, you know, cu-curious or whatever – experimenting." I sounded really dumb, but that's what you sound like when you're tongue's all thick and stuff.

Talia laughed. "C'mon, Dais, she's forty-five, for Christ's sake. She's not eighteen like you and me."

I was shaking a little, feeling the warmth of Talia's leg against my bare skin, feasting my eyes on all that porno, listening to all the rude things the brunette woman was saying to the blonde woman. And I just about jumped out of my skin when Talia suddenly put her arm around my shoulder.

She stared into my eyes and breathed, "You ever get curious, Daisy?"

I gulped. Talia rubbed my bare arm, and my body got all hot and tingly, a little lightning bolt shooting through my cunny. "Um, uh, well, I-"

She kissed me, all soft and warm and a little wet, right on the lips. I felt like I was melting. And when she pulled her head back, I sat there like a lovestruck dweeb, my eyes and mouth half-open.

Talia laughed, like it didn't mean anything. Then she pushed me away and jumped to her feet and said, "Take a look at this other shit I found."

I almost fell off the bed, but I held onto the magazine. Talia rummaged around in the closet, dragged out another box. I kept one eye on her and one on the magazine and one on the TV. The blonde was squeezing her big boobs and twisting her head from side-to-side, thrashing around on the bed and moaning and groaning while her girlfriend pumped her with the pink dildo, licked at her clitty.

Talia pulled a pink dildo out of the box and waved it under my nose. "There's all kinds of dildos and vibrators and junk like that in here," she said.

I nodded vaguely. Talia dropped onto the bed and playfully pushed the tip of the dildo against my lips. I opened up my big mouth and kind of sucked on the pink plastic.

And that changed everything. Everything got all serious all-of-a-sudden. I got real scared then – scared and excited, actually – realising what I'd done, and what I'd never done before.

I mean, I'd practice-kissed with a couple of girlfriends before – you know, just getting ready for the big moment with boys – but that was all just giggly, girly, innocent stuff. I'd never, ever gone seriously lezzy with a girl before. Never even really thought about it. But now, with those two beautiful women going at it right in front of me, and with beautiful Talia breathing down my neck, I wanted to experiment – like now!

I stared openly into Talia's dark, sparkling eyes, and she fed more of the dildo into my mouth. I sort of bobbed my head back and forth on it like I was sucking a boy's cock. Then Talia pulled the dildo out of my mouth, all wet and glistening, and stuck it in her mouth.

I could hardly breathe. Talia put her arm around my shoulder again. She slid the dildo out of her mouth, swirled her pink tongue all around it, and then slid it back into my mouth. I kind of quivered with excitement, feeling the incredible heat of the girl, her softness, my cunny gone so damp and squishy I thought I was going to wet the bed.

Talia glanced at the TV, and I followed her eyes, still sucking on the dildo. We both watched what the brunette was doing to the whimpering blonde with her pink dildo.

Then Talia shoved me back on the bed. She pushed my skirt up to my tummy, exposing my soaked panties, and I knew what she was going to do to me.

I held my breath, the blood pounding in my ears. Talia pushed my legs apart and touched my panty-covered cun with the dildo. "Yes!" I yelped, my body jumping. I grabbed on to the bedspread, shaking all over.

Talia rubbed the dildo against my electrified cunny, sending blazing sparks arcing all through me, setting me on fire, turning me wetter and juicier than I'd ever been before. Then she slipped a hand inside my blouse and grabbed onto one of my titties.

"Fuck, yes!" I hollered.

Talia grinned at me. She expertly popped my bra open at the front and covered one of my naked boobies with her warm hand, squeezed. I absolutely flooded with joy. I bit my lip and squeezed my eyes shut and let the wicked heat wash all over me. Talia stroked my pantied cunny with the dildo over and over, groping my boobs and rolling my blossomed buds between her fingers. And I took it and loved it, shivering with delight.

"I'm-I'm gonna cum, Talia!" I wailed.

"Nope, not yet, you aren't," she said. She pulled her hand out of my blouse, the dildo away from my smouldering cunny.

I scrambled up onto my elbows, squirmed higher onto the bed, as Talia gripped my sodden, heart-dotted panties on either side and yanked them down my legs. My face burned even brighter when I felt the warm air and Talia's eyes on my exposed coochie. My blonde fur was all shiny with moisture, my lips red and puffy with excitement.

Talia tossed my panties aside, then climbed on the bed and touched my bare cooch with the dildo. I jumped. The blonde on TV hissed, "Fuck me!" at her girlfriend, and I hissed, "Fuck me!" at Talia.

She plunged the dildo into my slit.

"Ohmigod!" I squealed.

Talia shoved the dildo all the way into my steaming cun. And that cocky pink thing was at least ten inches long! I almost squirted right then and there, but I managed to control myself – barely. Talia eased the dildo out of my slit, then plunged it all the way back in again. She started pumping me with the sex toy, grabbing one of my boobs and really pounding my slit.

I stared at her, all wild-eyed, my body rocking back and forth, my head spinning, my cunny buzzing with a warm, wet sensation I'd never gotten going solo. The blonde on TV suddenly screamed at the top of her lungs, her body jerking, girl juice actually jetting out of her cunny and into her lover's face.

I trembled out-of-control, a way-serious tingling building up in my cunny, pumping higher and higher with every stroke of the dildo. Talia fucked me faster, pulled on my buds. And when she lowered her head and licked at my clitty, it was so too much for me.

"Mmmm, yes!" I shrieked, tensing, then exploding. A humungous orgasm went off in my dildo-stuffed cunny and crashed through me. Quickly followed by a second, and then a third!

I gushed hot girly juice all over Talia's flying hand, onto her outstretched tongue, shaking like she'd Tazered my cunny. I totally lost it for a solid minute or so, fucked to the most awesome ecstasy ever by my wicked girlfriend, Talia.

I don't know if I passed out or what, but it seemed like a long, long time later that I felt someone kissing me –

kissing my boobs, nibbling on my nips. My eyes flickered open. It was Talia.

I pushed myself up onto my elbows and my head spun and I saw stars. I was all groggy-like, still glowing with the warmth of multiple orgasms. I licked my lips and was about to thank Talia for the truly wonderful experience when she said, "My turn."

I tried to focus, figure out just what she meant. Things got a whole lot clearer when she stood up and took off her blouse, peeled off her jeans. The girl didn't believe in underwear; she was totally naked!

I blinked my eyes and stared at Talia's skinny bod. Her titties were way smaller than mine, hardly more than a pair of bumps and a pair of cherry-red nipples. But those nipples were something, long and hard and pointing straight at me. Her cunny was shaved completely bare, her lips all pouty and slick-looking. She had a silver barbell in her bellybutton and a black butterfly tattooed on her lower tummy.

"Um, what do you want me …"

She pointed at the TV. The porno movie was amazingly still going, the blonde giving it to the brunette from behind with a strap-on dildo now.

I gulped. Talia grinned. Then the crazy chick lifted a black belt with a big, red dildo attached to it out of the box of goodies next to the bed. I'd never even seen a strap-on in-person before, let alone knew how to use one. Talia showed me.

She pulled me off the bed and fastened the belts around my hips and bum, the bright, red dildo sticking out ludicrously from my cunny. It felt weird wearing that thing, and a little loose. Talia cinched me tighter, and the dildo part pressed firmly against my cun. Then she dropped to her knees and started sucking on the foot-long cock.

"Yeah, um … suck me," I mumbled, totally unsure of myself. I kind of grabbed onto Talia's shiny hair and pulled her head closer.

She liked that. "Make me suck you off, bitch!" she hissed, staring up at me.

I jerked her head forward, and she gagged on the dildo, coughing and spluttering when I quickly pushed her head back. She attacked the dildo again, and I yanked her head forward again, forcing her to swallow my cock. I planted my feet and gritted my teeth and held her there, her cheeks bulging, her eyes watering and nose running. When I finally pushed her head back, she gulped and choked, the dildo popping out of her mouth all drippy and slimy with spit.

She sucked me some more, as I watched the women on TV, how the blonde gripped her girlfriend's waist and pumped her hips, pumped the brunette. My cunny got all tingly with the sight of those sexy women, with the friction of the strap-on rubbing me the right way as Talia sucked.

I pulled the girl's head up. "I'm gonna fuck you!" I growled, sounding all tough and experienced. I hadn't even had full-on sex with a boy yet, for gosh sakes, let alone with a girl.

Talia jumped to her feet and kissed me, stuck her tongue in my mouth and swirled it around. I got all warm and fuzzy, and I tried to grab her, french her back, but she wriggled out of my hands and dived onto the bed. She got up on all-fours and shook her skinny butt at me, daring me to do her.

I followed her onto the bed, my prick bouncing up and down like it had a life of its own. I kneed in behind her, put my hands on her bum, then stopped and tried to catch my breath. It was totally nuts – sweet little Daddy's girl Daisy getting ready to screw another girl with a strap-on dildo while hardcore lesbian porno played in the background. It was wild and crazy and absolutely wicked, and I went for it.

I gripped Big Red and shoved the tip of it into Talia's glistening cunny lips. I had to kind of feel around for her girl-hole for a second, but I found it. And when I did, Talia impatiently shoved back, burying the plastic prick to the hilt inside her.

The impact of her slamming ass-backwards against me sort of stunned me, rocked my cunny and my brain. Her smooth skin was hot against my skin, and I could smell her dripping cun. The strap-on moved against my own cunny as Talia wiggled her bum, and I got all damp and dizzy like before. Was I really, seriously going to have full-on sex with another girl? Yup, you bet I was! I started moving my hips, sliding my cock back and forth in Talia's stretched-out slit.

"Yeah, fuck me, bitch!" Talia yelled, twisting her head around and glaring at me.

I grabbed onto her waist like the woman in the movie and really pumped my hips. I got a smooth, fast rhythm going, slamming plastic cock into Talia's cunny, her lips gripping the pistoning dildo, my thighs smacking loudly against her rippling butt cheeks.

"Harder! Faster!" she screamed.

I went as fast as I could, digging my fingernails into her flesh. The dildo flew back and forth in her coochie, the bed creaking and banging the wall. Talia clawed at the bedspread, moaning, matching the ecstatic moans of the brunette on TV. Then she suddenly tensed up, muscles locking on her back and arms. I pounded her even harder, and she was jolted by orgasm.

"Fuck almighty!" she wailed, shuddering with ecstasy.

I kept right on fucking her – fucking her and fucking myself – the wicked friction on my clitty sending me sailing all over again. We came together, both of us totally blown away by the wet and wild ride.

It was when we were cleaning things up a bit that bad-girl Talia 'fessed up to the fact that she actually lived with her father, not her 'lesbian' mother. The porno magazines and DVD's were his, the many, many sex toys hers.

Come Dressed Up …
by Kitty Meadows

You'd be surprised if you saw me in my underwear. I don't seem the sort of girl who'd love garter belts and silky camisoles, shamelessly low-cut bras and frilly knickers. People might look at me and think, Hmm, matching white M&S cotton. But they'd be wrong. It's my one indulgence. I rarely drink and never smoke, I'm never overdrawn, I always remember birthdays and yes, even have a fully paid-up pension plan. I know to the outside world I seem pretty dull, but, secretly, I spend hundreds on my lingerie addiction and *almost* no one knows.

My ex-boyfriend and I used to plan mini-breaks around designer lingerie stores; we'd travel to Bath and Brighton, to Prague and Paris. I'd stock up on jewel-coloured negligees, G-strings and balcony bras with ruffles. I adored the little dressing rooms the shops always had and felt fearless inside their brocade-curtained cocoons. I'd boldly parade in front of him in soft little wisps of silk and lace knowing that when we got back to the hotel with the expensive bag with its expensive tassels swinging from my hand, I'd put it all on again and then he'd take it all off, very slowly and we'd have hard, hot, fast sex that would made me gasp and feel so good. Oh – and once we bought a waspie-waisted under-bust corset; and the sex! It was more passionate and exciting than ever. It was sex-in-the-movies sex! Head thrown back, eyes tight shut, mouth wide open and my whole body shaking with the kind of orgasm you only ever read about in books.

I love that corset.

I loved how it nipped in my waist, held my curves like an embrace, its shiny black satin cupping just under my breasts, pushing them up and scooping them juicily together. I loved the reckless girl I became in my corset, sexy, freed by the restriction of its severe cut, I was hyper-aware of the generous curves of my body reshaped into a cartoonish figure of eight and my breath was shallow when I was tightly laced into it. Best of all, I loved how powerful I felt when I wore it. Powerful but a little helpless too, which I guess was what made it so sexy.

As you can imagine, I'm on a lot of mailing lists and that night I'd been invited to the opening of a new lingerie store in the next town. I wasn't going to go. I was sad after the break-up, it had been a few months and I was in that stage where you're convinced you'll never have sex like that again; I went to my wardrobe and pulled out the corset. I closed my eyes and fingered its stiff satin, stroked the silvery clasps which fasted at the front and shivered at the memory. My eyes snapped open; sod it! I'd been so focused on work and I hadn't treated myself for months … a different town, going alone. Maybe this could be fun.

The invite said to '… come dressed up!' so I tried something I'd seen in a magazine. I wore one of my crisp short-sleeved white cotton blouses teamed with a nipped-in pencil skirt and fastened the corset over the top. I couldn't lace it too tight on my own but it looked great. I rifled through the hat box where I kept all my boudoir bits and bobs and secured a jewelled fascinator in my hair and finally slicked a bright scarlet lipstick, which I'd never dared wear out of the house, across my lips.

I looked in the mirror, could I really go out like this? I shrugged. Maybe this wasn't really me, I told myself, maybe it was the corset, making me behave badly!

In darkness I arrived at the shop, I could see it, all pinky lit, its windows festooned with gorgeous goodies. I parked nearby and in the shadow of a tree tugged my outfit together, re-applied my lipstick and then walked towards the shop. I tried the handle. Locked! I gingerly tapped at the door, waited a second and then walked away. I knew I should have stayed at home.

"There you are! So you could make it after all, but you're late!" cried a voice.

I turned around and in the doorway was an impatient-looking woman with the smallest waist I'd ever seen and the most amazing cleavage. She too, was wearing a white blouse with a black skirt and a jet black sequined bustier corset! But unlike me, she'd unbuttoned the blouse way past what I considered decent. I couldn't help gaping at her breasts. They were incredible, so creamily pale spilling out from her shirt. I looked down; maybe I could stand to undo just one button? At least I wouldn't look out of place. I smiled and walked towards her.

"Thanks so much for asking me, am I really late?" I said as I walked inside, "I thought it began at 8 p.m."

"Guests arrive at 9 p.m." she snapped. "I'm Nadine, you were meant to be here at 7 p.m., why did you say you couldn't come?"

"I didn't! I'm … I am a guest!" I told her, but she'd turned her back on me and was racing down the stairs.

14

"Hello?"

"Come ON!" she shouted, "Down here!"

I sighed and took a quick look around the shop, it was incredible, rack after rack of lacy bras and panties, a whole wall of spangled corsets and bustiers – oh, I couldn't leave, not without buying something.

"Are you coming?" the voice from downstairs shouted, so I cried out, "Yes!" and walked slowly down the stairs. I knew I should have stayed at home. I hated to draw attention to other people's mistakes, it always really embarrassed me.

I swiftly scanned the downstairs area, it was where they kept their toys; vibrators and butt plugs, anal beads and lube, my eyes whipped around the room and I could feel myself blushing. I tried to gather my courage together to explain to Nadine her mistake but stopped when I focused on what she was saying,

"… so as a new girl, you do, of course, get 50% off anything you want at the end of the night. Is that OK?"

"Half off?" I looked at her. "OK, what do I do?" Clearly whoever she thought I was wasn't coming, so I could get twice as much as I wanted upstairs. A bit of light shop work for an hour or two had to be worth it.

"Coat off, please." She held her hand out to me and then tutted and shook her head. "Who laced you into that? It's falling off! Turn around."

I meekly spun around and submitted to her ministrations. She began by loosening my corset and then she started to fasten me into it, far tighter than I was used to. I could feel my waist getting smaller and smaller but my tits were being jacked up absurdly, they were almost under my chin! They strained perilously under my buttons, I felt a little faint.

"Isn't that a bit tight?" I asked.

15

She laughed at me, "Funny girl, we're only half way there!" and she continued pulling the laces tighter and tighter. My hands fluttered down to feel my new shape. I was incredibly curvy, my waist just tiny, my hips swelled out sensuously and my breasts, oh God, I had no idea I could look like this at all. I was so entranced by myself that I barely uttered a word of protest as she swiftly undid three buttons so my cleavage too, was a voluptuous work of wonderment, just like hers.

"There." She nodded, "Now you'll do."

I turned around and looked at myself in the mirror. I didn't know the girl who looked back. She was sexy; she was so at ease with her body that she flaunted it to its best advantage, showing off her boobs, her bum and her hips. She was incredible. I took as deep a breath as I could manage. She was me!

"So, Lily, you're on toys tonight, have you tried the Excelsior range?"

I shook my head. Lily. That was a good name, certainly far more exotic than my own. Lily. I liked it. Nadine was now beckoning me over to a lavish display of vibrators, instead of the usual plasticky pinks and purples these were actually quite beautiful. They seemed to be made of glass with flower petals and gem stones captured inside. Curious, I picked one up; its end was gently curved, I hefted it, really – it was the width of a perfect cock – not too big, not too small. It was cool to the touch but quickly warmed from the heat in my hand.

"Gorgeous, aren't they?" she smiled. She leaned over and took it from my hand and turned the base, I could hear a buzzing sound. "They are unlike any others on the market, they look like glass but they're not, which is how come they can have a vibrating function too. Try it!" She passed it over.

I quickly held it to the back of my palm. "Um, lovely." I said. I was embarrassed; I didn't know how you were meant to try out a vibrator! Maybe this wasn't a great idea after all. I knew I should have stayed at home.

She laughed, "Not like that!" she took it from me and looked at me quizzically. "You haven't worked with me before, have you?"

I shook my head. "Then you really need to have a quick training session, we've got half an hour." She smiled impishly and boldly rubbed the tip of the vibrator across my shirt, teasing my breasts, I could feel my nipples instantly spring to life. Hugely embarrassed, I stepped away but backed into the wall.

"I don't, I mean, I'm not …" I trailed off. I didn't know where to go with that sentence. If I admitted who I was, how bad would that look? 'Hi, I'm here to get cheap stuff?' Better to try and pretend this wasn't happening, especially as my body seemed to have an agenda of its own. I could feel a familiar squirming inside; this was really turning me on. She began to circle my breasts with the vibrator, softly then harder, soft then hard, flicking at my erect nipples which were shamefully poking through my satin half-cup bra and pushing at my shirt.

"You can see that it's really a very fine product, you need to remember all this for when the customers arrive," she continued, "and, of course, that's just the start of the range. You carry on with that and I'll show you one of the others. She took my hand and placed the buzzing vibrator in it, mutely I carried on stroking my breasts with it. My face was on fire, I was probably the same shade as my lipstick, but she looked pleased.

"I think you'd be more comfortable if you sit down, don't you?" She gestured towards the ornate day bed in the corner of the room. It was covered in bras and half

17

slips, camisoles and garter belts. I awkwardly cleared a space and sat down and gasped when I looked at what sitting in the corset did to my breasts. Oh God, even bigger, straining even more against my shirt!

"In fact," she continued, "you'd probably be more comfortable if this was a bit looser, wouldn't you?" I assumed she meant my corset and nodded, but was amazed when she deftly unbuttoned my shirt and pushed my bra down so my nipples were fully exposed. She pulled the shirt down across my arms so it held them to my side.

Trapped!

I closed my eyes, if only I wasn't so turned on! I should just walk away but I couldn't. I'd fantasised about being with another girl but I'd never, you know, done *anything*. This was like a dream, a very wet dream, I could feel my best Myla panties getting increasingly damp and in a trance I deliberately flicked the vibrator across my bullet hard nipple and let out a small whimper.

It hurt.

It felt good.

What next?

She was now perched at my knees with three other vibrators. I felt like Goldilocks, one was far too big, one was too small and yes, there was one that looked just right.

"We'll start with the Excelsior Mini!" she said brightly, "Try to remember everything so you can tell customers later." Matter of fact, she pushed up my skirt and slipped an exploratory hand between my legs. "You're very wet," she observed, "I'm glad the agency sent me such a quick study. Some girls," she carried on in a confiding manner, "can't even get this wet no matter what you do. I'm very pleased that you can, it makes it

18

all a bit easier, don't you think?"

I was stunned into silence and hopelessly turned on; I could feel a snail trail of desire stickily dribbling through my panties. I didn't care what happened now, just so long as she touched my pussy, I was aching to be touched, to be filled up. I squirmed on the couch, eyes wide, waiting to see what she would do next. She took the smallest vibrator, pulled my legs apart and zipped it across the soaking crotch of my knickers and then she pushed it against my clit, slipped it under my pants so it rested directly against me. I cried out and she smartly pushed my legs together again, securing it buzzing away against me. I couldn't help but rock against it. I wanted more.

"This is the mini," she said, "it's perfect for playing with the clit and has three different speeds operating from this remote." She waved a slim box at me. "Slow ... medium ... and fast." The pulse between my legs throbbed harder, harder and then unbearably hard, I leaned back, unable to carry on stroking my breasts, I wriggled to get to the best position, I could feel an orgasm near but it kept slipping out of reach, I straightened my legs, crossed them, shifted desperately on the couch to try and pin it down.

She laughed, "You're going to work out great," Nadine beamed, "but you're a bit restless, aren't you? Let me help you with that." She got up and pulled my arms out of my shirt, then reached behind the couch and pulled out a pair of fluffy handcuffs, "Hands out!" she said. I was utterly her slave now; I'd do anything, anything at all, as long as she didn't stop. Mutely I reached my wrists towards her. She cuffed my right then tugged it behind my back, securing the left one too. Now I really was helpless, my breasts thrust out in front of me, rising and falling rapidly as my breath grew more and more shallow

19

thanks to the mini buzzing away busily between my legs. I didn't see how this was helping and was about to say so and beg for release when she pulled my legs apart again and, helping me stand up, tugged my knickers down. I shakily stepped out of them and then fell back on the bed as she reached up and laughingly pushed me over, I cried out in surprise and was stunned when she stuffed my pants in my mouth.

"That's better; I don't want you disturbing anyone." She winked and picked up the two other vibrators, looked at them both as she discarded 'just right' in favour of 'too big'. I pulled my knees together with trepidation but she just caught my left ankle in her hand and snapped a cuff on that too, linking the other end to the bed head board. I was now splayed open, vulnerable, arms caught behind my back and unable to protest as my mouth was stuffed with my muskily wet panties.

She picked up the mini from the floor where it had fallen and held it against my clit, my hips bucked as I finally got closer and closer to coming. I could feel the bigger vibrator in her hand now, stroking across my right thigh which I couldn't help but let fall, giving her complete access. I was focused completely on what would happen next. Surely it was too big? I could feel the tip nuzzling at my entrance, I was so wet, so swollen with desire that it easily slipped inside. I tensed and was amazed to feel it slide easily in and out, slowly and then faster.

"You see the maxi isn't as big as it seems if it's used in tandem with the mini," she intoned, "it does, however, have quite a strong vibrating pulse ..." she turned it on and my hips shot towards the ceiling, I screamed with pleasure and felt a wave of the hardest deepest orgasm crash over me, reducing me to mumbling, wriggling wetness. "… and it's shaped perfectly to hit that elusive G spot," she added.

That had to be it. I couldn't move, shackled to the couch, I was exhausted with pleasure. But no, she hadn't finished with me yet.

"Do you think you can persuasively sell those?" she asked. "You've seen their benefits?"

I nodded, coughing a little on my gag.

"Well, just one more to show you then and we're through." She picked up 'Just right' and grabbed a tube of lube too.

Now, I know some girls like their asses played with, but I'd never dared, it seemed too dirty, too rude to even think about. But I could see her lubing it up, a smile playing across her perfect lips.

"Let's untie you, make things a little easier," she said and undid my ankle. She gave it a thoughtful rub and then pulled me on to the floor beside her. I crashed down and she rolled me over, so I was on my side, cuffed wrists at my back with my skirt rolled around my waist, my knickers still stuffed in my mouth. I let out a squeal of protest and she stroked my hair.

"I don't believe in inflicting pain." She reassured me as I lay bound and gagged at her knees. She slipped a hand between my thighs and I felt the mini buzz into life again, "Not without enough pleasure to make it interesting, anyway." She added as an afterthought and reached behind me. I felt something cold and wet poke between my cheeks, oh God, I really wished I'd stayed at home. No discount could be worth this humiliation.

"Lily, this is the midi, you can use it alone or for best benefit, team it with the mini or maxi. You can probably tell by now that everything is easier, far less challenging if you just make everything else pleasurable enough. Oh

21

and relax!"

I felt my whole world boil down to just this: the essence of pure pleasure. My knees locked to hold the mini in place. It teased an exquisite and intense sensation from my clit which pulsed in waves around my whole body. I understood that if I relaxed, then the midi would slowly, insistently, slide inside my untouched ass and it wouldn't hurt. I could feel myself becoming full. So full. It felt unbearably humiliating but it was already impossible to contemplate ending it, I was alive with new sensations. The woollen rug rough against my face on the floor, the lace, soaked now, in my mouth, the feeling of the midi, in and out and in and out, I began pushing against it. I wanted more, I could feel myself losing control, I was shaking with the orgasm that was building and then there it was, I screamed and bucked, I felt my arse tighten, my thighs rigid I rolled on the rug and then, when it had shaken every part of me, it left me dizzy with unimagined pleasure.

She gently pulled the maxi out and stopped the mini. Flicked the panties from my mouth and uncuffed my wrists.

"I'll just give you 5 minutes to pull yourself together and then you can join the others upstairs. Just try and remember everything I've shown you and I'm sure you'll be fine." She looked at her perfect figure in the mirror, made some minute adjustment and then picked her way up the stairs without another word.

I lay bewildered, dishevelled and utterly satisfied on the floor. Every one of my prejudices had been shattered. I had experienced the most intense orgasm of my life at the hands of another woman who had explored parts of my body I had not even dared explore myself.

Come dressed up? I certainly had.

I groaned with pleasure. All this and 50% off. Thank God I hadn't stayed at home!

Belonging To Grace
by Lucy Diamond

Thank goodness it's 5 o'clock, I thought it was never going to arrive as I stood by the front door of the Sky Café praying no one would come in at the last minute. Luckily no one did and since I had become so skilled at closing up the shop, I cashed up, mopped the floor and pulled down the shutters within ten minutes. I love working at the Café, I enjoy chatting to the customers and larking about with the 'gang'. But tonight I feel exhausted and I'm glad that I only work there three days a week.

Initially I had only taken the job after university to earn some extra cash while I built up more freelance writing opportunities, but somehow six years later at twenty-eight I am still there. Don't get me wrong, I am not a total failure as a writer, I do regular pieces for a local paper and a couple of magazines; but I guess I am not the award-winning writer I dreamed I would be or that my girlfriend Grace would like me to be.

Grace is forever pushing me to try harder; to send my work out more and to try and make new contacts. She leaves me notes around our home before heading off to work: 'Lucy, don't forget to e-mail your "Blue River" chapters to Sally!' or: 'Lucy, take a look at this article;

it's nowhere near as good as your pieces?' Grace is a fully fledged 'type A'. When she left university she worked in a PR company for two years before deciding that she could make more money and have more fun running her own show so she and her colleague Ava set up their own company which they have been running for nearly eight years and which is hugely successful.

I feel really proud of Grace and what she has achieved; but on the downside it does mean I see less of her than I would like to. Also I have to put up with her seriously obnoxious colleagues and business customers. Ava in particular gets on my nerves, she is forever winding Grace up about my lack of motivation or 'life direction' as Grace has now taken to calling it. Ava and I have had many run-ins and now I generally try to avoid her unless absolutely necessary.

I am simply addicted to Grace. I love her, every part of her. I love her passion for life, her decisiveness, her smile, her strength and I even find her annoying habits tolerable (mostly). Grace and I have amazing talks but then she flips between understanding me and my life choices to allowing Ava to wind her up as I haven't finished my novel or that I have had a 'lazy' day.

All this animosity has stopped me from telling Grace that I have completed my novel but it was rejected by three publishers. Of course I feel enraged that Ava comes between us in this way and I often rise to Ava's bait when provoked, thus the whole avoidance strategy. Except tonight I have no choice but to spend the evening with Grace's work colleagues, Ava included, at a dinner party Grace is throwing in our home.

I have been worried about this party for nearly six weeks. When Grace first told me about it, I was unable to hide my dread, 'I cannot endure another bloody mind-numbing dinner party with your stuck-up, materialistic friends,' slipped from my lips as if against my will. Of course, Grace flipped out and she lectured me for so long that I would have agreed to anything just to get the telling off over with. Yes, my girlfriend was skilled at delivering a thorough dressing-down when she felt it necessary. 'Lucy, I have had about enough of your attitude *darling*,' that is how it would usually start.

Intense eye contact was Grace's thing. 'Look at me when I am speaking to you,' she would say while holding my chin up to force submission. I always felt she could run seminars and teach this skill to others, but having mentioned this to her a couple of years earlier during one of her rants at me, I ended up over her knee. And there is only one thing Grace is more competent at than scolding me, and that is delivering a very firm spanking.

This morning, I walked into the kitchen and found Grace standing at the door with her arms folded, looking very sexy in her black skirt suit and heels. Her blonde hair fell over her shoulders in what would appear to most to be a tousled look, but actually she had spent time sculpting this casual look to perfection. Her green eyes looked stern and before she even opened her mouth, a rush of trepidation washed over my entire body.

'Lucy, I want you to be on your absolute best behaviour tonight!' My God, I felt eight not twenty-eight but I knew better than to make any smart comments to her this morning. 'This is an important night for me and I want you to make an effort and get along with everyone and that includes Ava. This means a lot to me, do you understand me?' Grace asked.

'I promise, Grace,' I smiled my sweetest smile. Her face softened 'Good girl,' she said as she kissed my cheek. She picked up her bag and headed for the door as

26

she passed me, she gave my bottom a semi-gentle smack with the back of her hand and looked back at me with a wicked grin on her face, 'Let's hope that's the only swat your bottom gets today,' she said and then she was gone. A feeling of enjoyable discomfort burned in the depths of my stomach, causing my cheeks and neck to flush, God I love that woman!

I split my day into two halves and I spent the morning completing an article I have been putting off for weeks. Pushed by the deadline I become absorbed and six hours later I have posted off my polished and witty (if I do say so myself) contribution.

You see, I work best at the last minute, why can't Grace get that? Why does she think everyone should diarise and plan every detail? I print off my article to show Grace later, she loves to read my work. I spend the rest of the day getting ready, in amongst opening the front door to numerous caterers, florists, and Grace's PA, Callie, who, although only twenty-two years old, after working for Grace for nearly three years has turned into her very own mini-me. I leave them all to get organised executing Grace's detailed plans.

I take a long luxurious bath with candles, I exfoliate and moisturise my whole body and paint my toenails. I select a smart pair of figure-hugging sexy dark trousers and a red, scoop-neck, sleeveless blouse with killer heels. I pick out a new bra and panties set that I have been saving for a special occasion. I take extra long over my make-up and blow-dry my long chocolate-brown hair by section rather than my usual head upside down approach. 'Looking good, Luce' I say aloud as I check myself out in the 360-degree mirror.

When Grace arrives home, she comes into our bedroom and her eyes light up when she sees me. 'Wow baby, you look beautiful.' She pulls me by the hand over to the bed and sits me down on her lap. She runs her hand down my bare arm and kisses me deeply on my lips leaving me almost breathless. I want Grace so much right now, I want to jump into bed and make love to her with a sense of urgency. Grace breaks off from kissing me, 'Now remember, Lucy' she holds my chin up and looks me right in the eye, 'no nonsense tonight, baby, best behaviour you promised me.'

Grace got up and kissed my lips one last time and disappeared off to shower and get ready.

I watched Grace as she greeted her guests; she looked stunning and was especially sexy when taking charge of everyone and everything. I smiled to myself and she glanced over and caught my eye; she gave me a little wink and I threw her back my best smile.

The night passed with relative ease and I was seated (on purpose by Grace) at the opposite end of the table from Ava. I chatted easily to the other guests and mingled well afterwards. Grace would occasionally take my hand and lead me over and introduce me to various people. But instead of feeling like a trophy, I felt pleased she was so proud to be with me. 'Lucy is an amazing writer,' she beamed as she introduced me.

Some of the guests started to leave and I head out into the garden feeling happy I have successfully avoided Ava. As I speak to a few of the guests in the garden, I see Ava and Grace in the kitchen talking very animatedly, almost arguing. Ava is waving some documents at Grace who snatches them from her and seems to bark at her. I immediately head into the kitchen.

'What's going on, Grace?' I say, ignoring Ava. 'I could see you from the garden.'

Ava opens her mouth and Grace barks at her, 'Ava

28

don't even go there.' Ava walks out of the kitchen.

'What's going on, sweetheart?' I ask.

Grace didn't look me in the eye, she took the papers and walked towards the kitchen door, 'Nothing, Lucy, I'll talk to you about it later.' I didn't think too much about it at the time, I guessed perhaps it was a work problem.

After all the guests had gone, I noticed how quiet Grace had become; at this point she is usually drunk on her own success, fishing for compliments and wanting to replay each detail until I am too tired to talk to her.

But not tonight, tonight she is quiet but intense; I guess it's her argument with Ava that has troubled her. I have already been secretly congratulating myself that Ava did not manage to cause a rift between Grace and me tonight.

When we have finished cleaning up, I follow Grace into the bedroom. 'Baby, what's wrong, what's happened? Is there anything you want to talk over with me?' I say.

'No Luce, how about *you* tell me if there is anything that *you* want to discuss with me instead?' Grace says as she turns and looks at me her green eyes full of anger.

'I don't know what you are …' I stop in my tracks as Grace throws down the papers on the bed. I pick it up and my whole body shudders when I see the three rejection letters for my novel *Blue River*.

I immediately fathom that Ava has snooped amongst my belongings and has delighted in upsetting my girlfriend with the secret that has been eating away at me for a few months now. 'That devious, wicked cow,' are the first words I manage. 'She is trying to hurt us Gracie; she is trying to cause trouble for us.'

'I am not concerned with Ava or her scheming at all, Lucy.' Grace's voice is harsh and her anger cannot be hidden. 'It's you I have a problem with, Lucy, your dishonesty, your lack of respect for our trust, for our relationship.'

I feel sick inside. 'Grace, I just didn't want for you to be disappointed with me, I didn't want to let you down. I thought maybe I could fix this; I could make improvements and send it on to other publishers. I hoped you wouldn't have to know.'

'I am very disappointed with you, not because your novel wasn't picked up on the first attempt, I think that is fine. I am so angry and upset that you did not trust me to discuss it with me. You are supposed to share these things with me and talk it through.

I hate your dishonesty, that you have hidden this from me ... and for a while, going by the dates on the letters.' Grace's face and neck are red and she paces the room with her arms folded.

'I am so sorry, Grace, it's been chewing me up inside, I wanted to tell you. I really did,' I said with an aching heart.

'Am I that unapproachable, Lucy? What am I supposed to do with you? Tell me what the hell I am supposed to do with you?' Grace was nursing her rage, keeping it alive. 'Do you know what I am the most annoyed about, Lucy? I am just f**king furious and so humiliated to hear about this from Ava. That really pushes my limits, Lucy.'

I walk over to Grace and I go to take her hand, but instead she turns around and takes both of my wrists. She is not necessarily stronger than me in terms of physical strength but her hold over me is not a physical one alone. I look down and I feel my cheeks burning. 'I am sorry, Grace, truly sorry. I wish I had told you,' I say as the tears well up in my eyes.

'I am sorry too, Lucy, sorry that you chose the easy option again, sorry that you failed to do the adult thing, the responsible thing.' Grace lifted my chin up as she scolded me and looked deep into my eyes, causing a deep feeling of discomfort to churn deep in my stomach.

Grace didn't say another word; she kept eye contact and walked over to the bed.

She sat on the edge of the bed and stood me in front of her. My knees felt week and my head felt dizzy as I struggled to return her gaze. I searched her eyes looking for some warmth, looking for a way out of this but she gave me nothing in return and I dropped my gaze to the floor.

Grace's stare burned my cheeks as she watched me intently while unbuttoning my trousers and pulling them over my hips. With no verbal communication, she gestured for me to step out of my trousers. She gathered them up and threw them onto the nearby chair and brought her attention back to me as I stood on front of her. I wanted so much to climb on her knee and be cuddled and loved and forgiven but, after ten years together, I knew that was not the way that this would work out.

Grace pulled my pants down over my hips and they dropped to the floor. She stood up and raised my arms, pulling my blouse over my head and reaching behind my back to unclip my bra until finally I was completely naked. She sat back down and I stood in front of her. 'I'm sorry, Grace,' I said one last time looking into her eyes. 'I know,' she replied taking me by my left wrist and drawing me closer towards her. My knees were so weak I was ready to collapse in front of her.

'Lucy this is the last time you will ever lie to me or hide stuff from me. I love you more than life itself and I refuse to be shut out of your life in this way. Right now I am going to be more severe than I have ever been with you to try and make you understand this once and for all.' Grace's tone was stern and her steely determination was visible in her eyes and her posture. She gripped my left wrist more firmly and pulled my naked body across her knee.

The next couple of minutes seemed like an eternity, I am unsure what Grace was doing: whether she was composing herself, trying to heighten my anxiety or reviewing her approach. But I lay naked over her knees on our bed and my bare body shivered. I felt every sensation; I felt utterly exposed and helpless. I belonged to Grace in that moment and I was totally at her mercy.

'Are you ready, Lucy?' Grace asked.

'Yes,' I replied.

'Lucy I am going to spank you with my hand across your bare bottom until I feel you cannot take any more. I don't mind if you cry but under no circumstances are you allowed to get up or to interfere with this spanking. You understand?' Grace questioned me.

'Yes, Grace, I do.' The next thing I felt was Grace's hand crack down on my bottom, the first few spanks were not too bad, almost enjoyable even, but Grace delivered a series of spanks so thoroughly across my bottom and thighs that tears soon rose up in my eyes. She was unwavering in her vow to get her message across. 'Lucy, I hope as you lie across my knee' SPANK 'that you are thinking over why you find yourself in this position.' SPANK 'Again!!!' SPANK SPANK SPANK.

Grace showered my bottom with hard swats and the deep stinging sensation caused me to squirm across her knees. She seemed to know just what area of my bottom to bring her hand down on next, always seeking out the tenderest part of my burning cheeks. I felt tears trickle down my cheeks and my breaths became shorter as I gulped in air between each swat. Grace's breathing was also faster but she was dogmatic in her chastisement. She had to reposition me a couple of times as I was squirming to avoid the stinging print of her hand on my tender bottom. She punished my movement with harsh spanks to the inside of my thighs.

I let out my first squeal as she continued her diligent swats to my crimson bottom.

'Stand up, Lucy!' Grace commanded.

Finally, I thought. I stood in front of her, my bottom throbbed and my was face tear-stained. Grace looked me straight in the eye and wiped the tears from my cheeks. She then took my right wrist and yanked me back across her knee in the opposite direction to continue her assault with the other hand.

The pain was greater than anything she had inflicted upon me before. She kept it so painful that each spank throbbed but she didn't allow it to be so hard that my bottom went numb. She lifted my left bottom cheek slightly and started to spank the crease between my thigh and bottom, each spank landing with such intensity that I buried my head in the duvet and gripped the sheets tightly. 'I hope you are learning your lesson, Lucy darling,' Grace scolded me. She followed this with ten or so swats to the same area that caused me, against my will and better judgement, to bring my hand around and protect my bottom. 'Lucy!' Grace shouted at me and grabbed my wrist and held it across my back while spanking that area for harder and longer than I imagined I would be able to take. 'We will deal with your little misjudgement at the end, Lucy.' Grace chastised. She swapped over and lifted my other bottom cheek, allowing my hand to fall back to my side. She spanked me hard and then harder and I was now fully crying.

My bottom and thighs must have been scarlet by now and I lost any ability to control myself as I lay there. I thrust and squirmed about and Grace was constantly repositioning me. 'Lie still, Lucy. You need this, let every spank from my hand to your bottom deliver a message to your brain. I never want you to forget this spanking.' Grace was so strict; she had never been so tough on me. She spanked me for another few minutes as I sobbed over her lap, my body was limp, my heart pounded and the heat in my bottom was fierce. Grace finally stopped.

She made no move for a few minutes and neither did I. She did not touch or rub my bottom and thighs as she usually did to comfort me. I daren't turn around for fear of her gaze. I wondered how I must appear to her as she looked down on me.

Finally she speaks, 'Lucy, I want you to get up and go to the corner.'

What the hell, I think to myself, I want to say to her that I don't want to do that and that I want my cuddle and to go to bed with her, but I don't. I get up and walk across our bedroom to the corner and stand in the corner. I stand for a long time, I am unsure how long but possibly it is around twenty minutes.

For a while I feel Grace sitting on the bed watching me in silence. But she leaves the room and comes back and I hear her moving about but I am unsure what she is doing.

'OK, Lucy, come to me, please.' Grace's tone is still strict and as I walk to her I see she is holding a wooden paddle and she has positioned two cushions in the middle of the bed. 'Lucy, I want you to lie face down and place your bottom over the cushions as if they were my knee,' Grace requests. As I go to comply Grace, stops me for a moment and holds my chin up and we look into each others eyes. Her stare is intense and sends a quiver of excitement to my deepest core and I blush.

I climb onto the bed and position myself over the cushion. 'Lucy, I am going to paddle your bottom for 20 swats,' Grace advises me as if telling me a piece of trivia from the morning papers. I want to shout out that I can't take it but I lay still and wait.

The first crack of the paddle over my bottom is intense and stings, the corner time was enough to cool it down just a little so the numbness disappeared and the paddle started its tirade of cracks against my red raw bottom. On the second crack I cried out.

'I hope you will never hide anything from me again, Lucy.' CRACK, CRACK. 'I want to be able to trust you,' CRACK, CRACK, CRACK, 'I love you, Lucy, you're my girl.'

CRACK, CRACK, CRACK CRACK CRACK. 'I am doing this for you.' CRACK, CRACK, CRACK. 'I have decided that I am going to become far more involved in helping you have at the very least a basic writing plan in place,' CRACK CRACK CRACK, 'to combat your persistent procrastination.' CRACK CRACK CRACK. Each swat throbbed and my legs flew about wildly as I gyrated on the cushions trying to avoid the force of Grace's paddle. Grace swung her arm so far back that the last swat was so fast and hard that the noise as it cut through the air was audible: WHOOSH, CRACK!!

Grace had beaten me harder than ever and for the first time since the dinner party the tenderness returned to her voice. 'Are you OK, Lucy? Have you learned a lesson?' She doesn't expect an answer at this point she moves and sits next to my body and she rubs my bottom gently and then harder. She rubs each cheek and thigh and works her way inside my thighs. She rolls me over gently and I wince as my bottom is pushed against the sheets. She looks into my eyes and smiles as she watches me wince. 'I love you, Grace, I'm so sorry!' I say through a teary voice. Grace kisses me and her relentless hands move down my stomach and in between my legs as she begins to work her magic all over again.

I feel safe with Grace.

Siren
by Beverly Langland

Colleen turned away briskly trying to avoid the angry water as the wave broke over the bow. Too late – the cold spray caught her full on. She shook her head, cleared her eyes the best she could before turning back to the helm, edging her charge a little closer to the wind. Elizabeth looked on anxiously but visibly relaxed once she realised the young woman was smiling through the mass of black hair plastered to her face. *Who would have dreamed this time last week I would be sailing*, thought Colleen. *Me of all people! And not just sailing but in charge of the tiller*. Then a lot had changed in seven days. She was no longer the frightened timid shop-girl. Together, she and Elizabeth had set forth on a great adventure. Already she was filled with a sense of excitement, of fear, though her trepidation had little to do with the vast waters around her, nor the fierce wind lashing at her face. Her anxiety came from the Siren known as Elizabeth. Colleen glanced at the older woman as she set about the business of keeping Adriana afloat. Her outward calm belied the ferocity of the storm, belied the fierce passion hidden beneath the surface. Yet it had started so peacefully ...

As Colleen peered from behind her novel she thought them both beautiful. Adriana with her sleek, elegant lines and the auburn-haired woman, serene and sophisticated as she sipped cocktails or lay sun-bathing along the bow. Colleen observed them each day from the safety of her hotel balcony. She knew she should be more adventurous, should explore further than just the beach immediately in front of the hotel with its small marina. That's what the holiday was all about, after all – a new start, a new determination to forge her own path. Colleen felt she was different to most girls. Well, not *that* different – she still craved companionship, still hoped to find love. Trouble was she lived with her parents in a small rural village. Residents there held fixed opinions, couldn't understand why she had not yet married, had not started a family of her own.

Hence the holiday; a time to reflect, the chance to meet someone of similar mind. Though Colleen hadn't yet ventured far from the hotel. Something about the woman on the yacht constantly drew her attention – like a Siren calling to her, demanding her attention. Colleen felt unnerved by her compulsion to watch, a little thrilled by her new found voyeurism. Enough! She had to break free of her lethargy. Tomorrow she would explore one of the coastal villages. Though strolling through the marina, her temptation to loiter as she passed Adriana became too great to resist. She looked around. There was no sign of the woman. Colleen paused, imagined what it must be like to own such a yacht, to have the freedom to sail into the distance, to not look back. At that instant, the red-headed woman appeared in front of her, eyes wide, curious. Colleen realised the woman had been crouched in one of the lockers and she had not noticed. The Siren flashed a smile, bright as the sun overhead. "Hello."

"Hi. I was just …"

"Beautiful isn't she?"

"Very."

"You know much about boats?"

"Nothing actually."

The beautiful face turned suddenly dark, the pupils of the green eyes shrinking to pinpoints. "So it's me you've been spying on from your watchtower!" She pointed towards Colleen's balcony. "Bloody paparazzi. Can't you people leave me alone?"

"I wasn't. I mean I'm not …"

"A likely story!"

"Honest. I have nothing to do with the press."

"But you *were* watching me?"

Colleen blushed, decided to ignore the question. "Are you famous then?"

The woman's anger dissipated as her amused smile developed into a full-blown laugh. Colleen felt herself turn a deeper shade of red. Should she have recognised this woman?

"No, not at all. The name's Elizabeth." She held out a slender hand.

"Colleen."

The two women shook hands politely, Elizabeth holding on a moment as if considering options. "Would you like to come aboard, Colleen?" Elizabeth shaded her eyes with the palm of her hand, momentarily surveyed the horizon before turning to face Colleen once more. "Not much chance of a sail, I'm afraid, but I was considering motoring to a quiet cove not far from here. We can picnic if you like."

Colleen felt a little stunned. One minute the woman was berating her, the next inviting her on to her boat. Still, the opportunity seemed too good to pass, and besides Colleen still felt that strange compulsion to stay close. "Sounds wonderful." She examined the clothes she wore. "Should I change?"

Elizabeth eyed the young woman. "Dress code aboard the Adriana is *strictly* casual."

"But I don't even have my bikini."

Elizabeth smiled again. "Don't worry, you won't need one. The cove I have in mind is isolated. Few tourists venture that far from the beaten track."

"And the locals?"

"The odd goat perhaps. It's too far from the road for the locals to bother in this heat. I'm afraid you'll have to suffer my company."

Though excited, once aboard Colleen felt awkward and out of place. She had no idea what was going on as Elizabeth calmly and efficiently cast off and manoeuvred Adriana away from the marina and out into the bay. All Colleen could do was watch in wonder as individual figures on the beach slowly melded into one colourful mass. Soon even the mass faded and all she could see was a sun-hazed shoreline. She turned her attention to Elizabeth. Colleen watched as the older woman moved – lithe as a cat – from one task to the next. Elizabeth glanced up, caught Colleen's scrutiny. "I wish I could help," Colleen said, in an effort to hide her pleasure in watching Elizabeth move.

"You can help stow these," Elizabeth answered, passing Colleen a fender.

Once they had finished Elizabeth sat next to Colleen in the cabin. "You can relax now. Why don't you strip down to your undies? No one will notice."

Colleen blushed again. "My bra and knickers don't match."

"Go topless then. I normally do."

Colleen hesitated, for some reason she averted her eyes as Elizabeth removed her bikini top, even though exposing one's breasts appeared to be the norm on the hotel beach. Perhaps she simply wanted to see them too much and couldn't bear the burden of guilt she felt. Elizabeth waited. "Go on. You're on holiday. Besides, there are only us girls all alone out here." There was the call again, urging, luring. Still, Colleen remembered her resolution. "Yes. I *am* on holiday!" She stripped to her panties; hoped Elizabeth wouldn't notice her nervous trembling, notice how erect her nipples were.

There was no chance of that. Elizabeth seemed to watch her every movement, stared openly at the girl's breasts. "It's the sea breeze," she said nonchalantly. Colleen's flush spread to her throat and chest. Elizabeth smiled warmly, a twinkle in her eye. "I love the way you blush so readily."

"Do I?"

For a long while Colleen sat forward, her hands squashed between her thighs, arms hiding her nipples. When she realised that Elizabeth paid her no attention she relaxed, lay back against the cushions, enjoying the warmth of the sun on her skin. They motored to the secluded cove with hardly a word spoken, the sound and vibration of the diesel engine lulling Colleen into a state of semi-consciousness. Behind her closed eyelids she thought only of Elizabeth, of Elizabeth's sun-tanned body, of the freckles on the woman's breasts.

"You should put on more sunscreen."

Colleen sat up, pleasantly dazed, to find Elizabeth edging Adriana into a horseshoe-shaped cove surrounded on all sides by high cliffs. Elizabeth placed the engine in neutral, dropped anchor, drew in the chain using the motorised hoist until the anchor caught and the chain became taut. Satisfied, she cut the engine. After the gentle drone of the previous hour the silence was striking. Colleen looked around wide-eyed. The cove looked idyllic, the surrounding hillsides deserted, the only onlooker a somewhat bemused goat, and even he moved on.

Elizabeth was in the turquoise clear water before Colleen had fully taken in the spectacle. "Come on! The water's lovely."

After some hesitation Colleen followed. It wasn't an elegant dive and in the process she lost her panties. She thrashed around in a minor panic trying to find them.

"These yours?" Elizabeth teased, holding aloft the sodden material. She swam over to the younger woman. "Feels good doesn't it? Swimming naked, I mean."

"Yes," admitted Colleen.

Elizabeth took hold of Colleen's hand, guided it between her legs while she effortlessly trod water. She looked deep into the girl's eyes. "I left mine on deck."

"Oh." Colleen felt her cheeks flush again.

Elizabeth pressed hesitant fingers against her sex. "You know, I don't believe you're as innocent as you make out Colleen. You realise – or suspect now at least – why I invited you on board?"

"No. I mean ..."

"Hoped perhaps? Why else did you spy on me, day after day?"

"I wasn't spying."

"Come now, we both know that you were. Don't be shy – tell Lizzie the truth. Do you like to watch other girls? Did you touch yourself while you watched me?"

"No!"

"Not your type?" Elizabeth wrapped her lithe legs around the girl's waist, clasping her tightly.

"Please, I'm not a strong swimmer. I'd like to go back now."

"Of course."

Back aboard the Adriana, Colleen busied herself with the pretence of towelling dry, with applying sun-screen lotion.

"Here, let me do that."

Colleen nervously handed Elizabeth the bowl of oil and lay passively on her front as Elizabeth began to rub the oily lotion into her skin. Her hands felt soft and sure and soon Colleen fell back into her languid state. Then, without a word, Elizabeth straddled Colleen's legs, sitting just below her bottom. Colleen was intensely aware of Elizabeth's nakedness. Her sex felt hot and moist against her skin. As the woman worked her way from shoulder to legs, her hands lingered on the girl's bottom, slick fingers dipping between those cheeks, teasing, delving between her thighs and the backs of her legs.

"God, that feels good," Colleen said, then opened her eyes wide in alarm. "I can't believe I just said that out loud!"

"Don't worry, I feel the same. I can't remember the last time I …"

"Eight months," Colleen admitted.

"With a girl?"

"With anyone."

"You poor thing."

Elizabeth expertly massaged oil into Colleen's skin. Her fingers found the two dimples on Colleen's lower back; her hands sculpted the swell of Colleen's hips, the curves of her bottom, the depth of her cleft. Colleen spread her legs slightly as Elizabeth continued to massage her upper thighs. She began to fret when she realised that in so doing she had exposed her sex, perhaps her puckered brown anus. She imagined Elizabeth

43

exploring there, bending close, probing deep with her tongue. The notion made her tingle.

Suddenly Elizabeth slapped Colleen's thigh as if reading her wicked thoughts. "Roll over!"

Slowly, Colleen turned onto her back. She shielded her eyes from the glare of the sun only to be confronted with Elizabeth's inquisitive green eyes. A little of the initial playfulness had gone, replaced now with a look of undiluted passion. As if to please her tormentor, Colleen blushed when she realised she stared directly at Elizabeth's sex. The way Elizabeth straddled her had parted her lips. They looked inflamed and bloated.

Elizabeth reached into the bowl, brought her hands out shiny and dripping with oil. She rubbed them together, then caressed her breasts, smoothing the oil over her skin until she shone softly in the sunlight. More oil and her hands moved downwards over her flat tummy, her hips, her upper thighs. Again more oil, this time she reached to caress Colleen. She began at the girl's feet, working up her shins and thighs, deliberately skipping Colleen's mons, though she briefly teased her sex with a trailing finger before moving on to the girl's quivering belly. Then her hands sidetracked to Colleen's arms, her shoulders, before again edging inwards.

Colleen knew full well Elizabeth's game. Certainly, the Siren made no pretence of her ultimate goal. Once more dipping her hands into the warm oil, she placed them on Colleen's breasts, making the girl's nipples stand to attention like two pink sentries.

Slowly Elizabeth shifted position, leaning ever closer until her nipples brushed against Colleen's breasts. Oiled skin against oiled skin, she slid lower, the pressure light but the contact unbroken. Lower and lower, then back up until her breasts hung above Colleen's face. Elizabeth slithered from side to side, rubbing Colleen's breasts with her stomach, her own breasts dangling tantalisingly close to the girl's mouth. Aroused, Colleen felt suddenly emboldened. "I think you missed a spot," she whispered. Elizabeth sat upright, looked a little puzzled until Colleen spread her legs slightly, raising her head to look directly into Elizabeth's eyes.

Elizabeth smiled wickedly. "Yes, I believe you're right. Such a tender spot deserves special attention." She gathered more lotion onto her fingers, rubbed it into Colleen's already shining wet labia. Her long, graceful fingers danced over the girl's sex, teasing her protruding clitoris, occasionally probing into the opening as Colleen's expectant lips slowly parted. Colleen shifted her hips a little, insinuated one of her feet against Elizabeth's sex, wriggled her toes into the moist gap. She could feel Elizabeth, wet and so hot she was like a furnace against Colleen's own skin, and her eyes were glistening and wet. Elizabeth dropped her foot behind the wooden railing and pushed forward. The deck locker squeaked as Colleen gently rocked her hips, pushing towards Elizabeth's fingers, seeking the illicit touch. Elizabeth rocked with her, pelvis pressing downwards, riding as if she was on a horse, grinding herself against Colleen's foot, then sliding onto her shinbone. Elizabeth made soft sounds, her hips moving with increasing urgency, all the while her fingers played along the folds of Colleen's pussy, slipping underneath, making her move her own hips.

"I want to fuck you," Elizabeth said, her voice suddenly full of want. Hearing those words from Elizabeth's soft lips filled Colleen with fire.

"Yes, fuck me," Colleen agreed, gasping then as Elizabeth's fingers probed further, as, for a moment she buried them completely. Then the wonderful fingers were gone and Colleen felt Elizabeth's weight shift again.

She waited patiently, wanting, needing, as Elizabeth rooted in the locker and came out with a bright red … sausage-shaped dildo? At first Colleen felt a little confused, moved pliantly as, little by little Elizabeth reposition herself, worming her way between Colleen's spread thighs, pulling at her hips until her pussy came into contact with the girl's own heated sex, two intertwined scissors. Colleen watched with increasing trepidation as Elizabeth positioned the dildo at the entrance of her sex, pushed, swallowed greedily. "Now you," she whispered, gently prodding Colleen's wetness with the other end of the dildo. Colleen bore against it, letting the soft rubber fill her, pushing until her inflamed lips once more kissed Elizabeth's.

"With me," were Elizabeth's only words as she pressed deeper on to Colleen. Colleen responded, filled with awe at this newly discovered pleasure. Soon the two found a beautiful rhythm, mashing together until they became a swamp of heat and desire. It took only a little while before Colleen discovered she could crush her clitoris against Elizabeth's pubic bone. Each exquisite 'bump' brought forth a tiny whimper. On and on the two gyrated, each encouraged by the groans of the other. The slap of wet flesh against wet flesh, the wicked squelching of the dildo breaking through drove Colleen crazy. She rapidly picked up the pace; frantically racing towards the release denied her for so long.

"Not yet," Elizabeth pleaded, "I'm not ready."

"I'm so wet, so hot!" Colleen couldn't stop whatever Elizabeth's wishes. Her body moved by itself, rubbing, pushing, gyrating, fucking. She clenched her bottom cheeks – hard – trying to hold off, trying to back away. It was no use. She wanted to be as close as possible, closer than they already were, to be inside Elizabeth somehow, to share what she felt with her, to know what Elizabeth felt as she pushed deeper. She pumped harder, forcing their burning flesh into angry collision, wanting to merge with her lover, wanting to siphon Elizabeth's heat. Colleen looked up and the two locked eyes. Elizabeth's expression had changed, she looked happy and worried at the same time, looked a little worried perhaps, Colleen thought, as if she were frightened of losing control. Elizabeth's cheeks burned red, her eyes glazed for a moment, then they grew as wide as saucers and her whole body started to tremble. "Oh, fuck …"

Colleen felt Elizabeth's body jerk suddenly, just as her own began to spasm. She felt as if a fist had grabbed her between the legs, the softest, most gentle fist imaginable, Neptune's fingers, grabbing her right there inside, shaking her, turning her inside out. She felt a strong throbbing between her legs like nothing she'd felt before. Colleen couldn't think, or talk, couldn't do anything except close her eyes, hold on until the tremors passed; her orgasm so intense it almost hurt when she finally let go.

Gradually, breath seeped back into her lungs, her heart started to beat once more, though her blood continued to burn. Colleen tingled all over. She didn't want to move, so she lay quiet, gently stroking Elizabeth's leg, enjoying her heat, their sex still pressed together. She didn't know exactly what had happened. She'd felt good before, but never quite like this. Slowly, she raised herself on to her elbows. Elizabeth sat up too. The older woman smiled but her eyes were wet, her flushed cheeks glistening with tears. Colleen wanted nothing more than to hold Elizabeth in her arms, to be held, to be kissed by those soft pink lips. She knew there would be time enough for romance. She had the whole summer, longer …

Colleen lay back a little, feeling the glorious heat on her skin, listening to the waters gently lap against the hull of the yacht. She felt so alive. She began to caress her breasts with both hands, her fingers tracing circles on her oiled skin, moving inwards to her nipples, pulling them, rolling them between her fingers, releasing, then circling outwards again. After the passion of the last few minutes she enjoyed the teasing sensation. Soon one hand snaked over her stomach, circling, brushing through her short pubic hair, delving between her lips, between Elizabeth's lips. For a long moment she teased herself, teased Elizabeth. Elizabeth moaned softly, brought her own hand to join Colleen's. From then on they worked in tandem.

Soon Elizabeth began to rock gently, panting, making small soft sounds. Colleen moved with her, edging closer, falling into rhythm, her passion rising once more. "Fuck me again," Elizabeth pleaded. Colleen happily obliged. It seemed she had made a decision. Colleen wasn't catching the charter flight home, wasn't going anywhere soon. The Siren called to her and willingly Colleen threw herself onto the rocks.

Blood And Bliss
by DMW Carol

The beat was pounding, thump, thump, thump: a primal call to get on your feet and surrender to the music. The room would have been dark save for a flickering strobe light that illuminated the artwork scrawled on the walls and threw the dancing bodies into sharp relief. Their abandoned movements were intoxicating and eerie in the half-light, almost hypnotic. The club was busy, the music was raw and it was hot.

I wasn't sure I'd find what I was after here. Hunting a Goth club was a fun cliché, but it wasn't stocked with the sad lone waifs you might expect. The club was full of happy laughing crowds of lively people, a constantly moving sea of black lace and make-up. Everyone seemed to know everyone else and there were more squeals of laughter, people demanding hugs and people collapsing in giggles than enigmatic loners wafting tragically around like their one true love had just died of consumption or belladonna poisoning. Still, there was some serious eye candy to be admired and it wouldn't hurt to watch for a while.

I walked over to the bar and selected the least objectionable sounding of the red wines. A 2004 Minervois, spicy and with a hint of fruit, definitely palatable although not my usual taste. While the barman was pouring it for me I selected one of the high stools which offered a good view of the dance floor.

I crossed my legs and settled back to enjoy the view. To be honest, it was good to rest my feet, the boots looked fantastic but heels that high are never comfortable for long and I could feel the ache starting to gnaw. It was worth the discomfort, though, I knew that I looked fantastic. I'd taken special care getting ready and could hold my own against any of the pretty boys and girls in the club. The tight-laced purple silk corset accentuated every curve and cradled my breasts like the hand of a lover. Under that a short, flared, black skirt, with layers of ruffles, laced together over stiffened net petticoats edged with deepest purple, black suspender belt, seamed black fishnet stockings, and a riding jacket of black velvet lined in purple silk. My hair was hidden under a purple wig which swung to below-shoulder length and perfectly complemented the corset. I wore more jewellery than usual – all silver, of course. I'd spent ages perfecting my make-up, my eyes were dark and sultry, and for once I didn't try to hide my porcelain-white skin; the final touch was a coating of lip gloss, rich, dark and inviting, like a succulent black cherry.

I sipped my wine and scanned the crowd. You certainly couldn't fault the view, pretty girls, short skirts, fancy boots, this place had it all in abundance. Some of the men were almost as pretty. The styles ranged from ruffles and lace to rubber and chrome, Victorian gothic to futuristic cyberpunk. It felt strangely welcoming. Even the music was good. I'd give it a while longer before I had to take care of business.

Then I saw her. She'd only just arrived and was making her way towards the bar scanning the crowds as though hoping to spot a familiar face on her way through the club. She was petite, blonde and with deep blue eyes that reflected the flickering light like pools of clear water. Her skin was almost as pale as my own. She was dressed in a floor-length white dress that glowed in the UV lighting. Her slim waist was cinched with a red velvet waspie and beneath the handkerchief hem I caught the occasional glimpse of black patent-leather high-heeled boots. A thin red ribbon encircled her neck centred with a with a clear quartz point cocooned with a dragon. She looked angelic. She had a kind of frailty about her that made her look vulnerable and incredibly desirable. She signalled to the barman and I smiled when she too ordered the Minervois. Our eyes made contact, there was a spark there, she seemed to instinctively know that I wanted her and she held my gaze for about ten seconds. I raised my glass in salute and saw her pale cheeks colour slightly before she smiled faintly and looked down at her wine.

I stood up and walked around to where she stood. In my heels I was a good few inches taller than her and she looked up at me and dared a tentative smile.

"May I join you?" I asked, sitting down next to her. "I'm Serena, I've not seen you here before …"

"I'm Aimee," she replied, with a tremor to her voice. "Please do join me, I don't really know anyone here and it would be good to have someone to talk to."

I looked at her carefully. Despite her slender figure she had beautiful full breasts that were barely contained by the sweetheart neckline of her dress. Her eyes were even more startling close up and they hardly needed the smoky smudge of kohl that surrounded them. Her lipstick was vivid scarlet and I swear I had never seen anything more kissable in all my years.

"To darkness and light," I said clinking our wine glasses together. "Your light and my darkness."

She smiled at that. "A perfect contrast," she agreed with me.

We drank our wine and I ordered a bottle so we wouldn't be distracted by needing refills. I asked Aimee about herself. She was an artist, not long out of university and struggling to get established. She lived alone and didn't really socialise that much. She had come to the club tonight because she felt drawn to the Goth scene, inspired by the poetry and romance, and was hoping to make a few friends. I probed deeper, asking if she had boyfriends.

"No." She shook her head. "No boyfriends." She looked evasive and a faint blush bruised her cheeks.

I smiled. "Girlfriends, then?"

"Well," she hesitated, then carried on, "not at the moment, but I've had one or two in the past. I just don't seem to get on well with boyfriends, really."

I smiled at her. "I prefer women too. There's something so soft and inviting about them, you just don't get that with men."

I let the subject drop, but we carried on chatting. The talk flowed comfortably. Maybe it was the wine but something was working magic on Aimee, she became less nervous, more open and when I occasionally brushed against her she smiled at me with a good amount of interest. Her cheeks were colouring to a rosy pink, whether from the wine or from her rising passion, I couldn't be sure, but I had my hopes.

When I was as sure as I could be, I placed my hand over hers as it rested in her lap and held it tight.

I knew I hadn't read things wrong when she turned towards me, obviously expecting to be kissed. Her lips parted slightly and she leaned towards me, I dipped my lips to hers and savoured that first taste. We held like that for a perfect moment before her lips parted further and I slipped my tongue between them. I was delighted at how willingly she responded. We kissed for a minute or so, I could feel my nipples harden under the satin of my corset and the heat begin to build in my groin.

She pulled away from me.

"Oh Serena," she whispered. "I want you so much."

I nodded and smiled at her. "I want you too. We could go to my place. It's not far and then we could really get to know each other properly."

We left the club and were lucky enough to find a cab almost immediately, it wasn't even a surprise when the driver knocked a couple of quid off the fare – he'd spent more time watching the two of us kissing and cuddling than watching the road. I figured he'd be talking about the two hot Goth chicks who made out in his cab for weeks. We put on a good enough show to fuel a whole host of fantasies but kept the reality just within the bounds of decency. I always perform better when there isn't an audience to worry about.

By the time we reached my apartment I could tell that our little show had got Aimee's pulse racing as well as the taxi driver's. As for me, well, my mind was running in overdrive choosing exactly what to do next in my mission to bring her to total ecstasy.

I led her straight to the bedroom. This was no time for subtlety and I could see no reason to miss out on the comforts my opulent chamber could provide. It said everything I needed to hear when she stepped willingly into the room. I'm proud of my bedroom, the décor captures my nature perfectly. It's a hedonistic palette of rich jewel tones and sumptuous fabrics. I think that the blood-red walls, velvet drapes and four-poster bed are the perfect scene for seduction.

I pulled Aimee into a tight embrace and kissed her full on the mouth again, I felt her relax into the kiss. My hands roamed across her back, sweeping ever lower as she pressed into me. I ran a fingernail down her spine and felt her shiver. My hands dropped to her waist and continued lower, following the curve of her buttock and grasping it through the fabric of her skirt.

She responded with a similar caress, only my skirt was shorter and her hands slipped naturally below it. I heard her sigh as she realised I was naked under the short skirt and parted my legs just enough for her to feel the heat from my eager pussy.

I trailed kisses down her neck as I opened the bodice of her dress, letting her breasts spill out into my hands, they were full and round, perfectly white and crowned with perfect rosy pink nipples and areolae. I kissed each breast in turn, feeling her tremble with pleasure as I began to suckle. She really was delicious and I couldn't wait to taste all that she had to offer.

We dropped onto the bed, still dressed. Our limbs entwined as we resumed kissing and caressing. As we rolled together the skirt of Aimee's dress crept higher and I was soon able to reach below to explore the tender skin exposed above her white lace stocking tops and to begin to explore the soft silk that clung to the cheeks of her bottom.

I rolled her on to her back, with the dress bunched up around her waist and quickly slipped the white knickers down over her hold-ups. I pulled them clear and let them drop to the floor as I admired the precious treasure they had been hiding. She was exquisite in her nakedness, her smooth pubic mound was so enticing and her pink pussy lips were inviting my kiss.

I knelt beside her and parted her lips with a fingertip, feeling the warm wetness inside. She moaned louder as my fingertips found her clit, I traced a lazy circle around the perfect bud and felt it swell under my touch. She moaned and I looked up, eager to see her enjoying the pleasure I was giving her. She looked utterly abandoned as she writhed to my touch. Her hands were circling her breasts, her eyes were shut and her mouth parted with a moan as I stepped up the stroking and teasing of her wet pussy. Her knees were raised and her legs parted wide as I began to probe deeper inside her. It was difficult to tear my eyes away from her surrender, but I dipped my head and began to lap at her clit, like a kitten licking cream from a fingertip.

Slowly I increased the pressure, licking harder, my tongue pressing her swollen bud against my teeth, sucking it into my mouth and even nibbling gently at this tender fruit. Simultaneously my fingers thrust into her wet chasm, in and out, faster and harder with every stroke. She gripped my fingers tightly with her pussy muscles, gasping with the pleasure of my ministrations.

I knew that she was close to orgasm, her breathing loud and ragged, her back arched as she pushed hard against me, her thrusts matching my own. When she came she cried out, gasping my name over and over again.

My pussy was throbbing with excitement, my juices flowing and making my thighs wet and sticky. I withdrew my fingers and licked them clean of her juices, savouring their sweetness.

As I relaxed back on to the bed, it was Aimee's turn to take control. She knelt between my legs, her mouth on my pussy, her tongue probing inside me, penetrating me and withdrawing then circling around my opening and darting back inside. She had one hand holding my lips open while the fingers of her other hand rolled and pinched my clit.

As she lapped at my juices her fingers began to drum against my clit. Her tongue danced over my pussy, darting inside with short little thrusts, flicking up to my clit and then back. I was lost in the moment, aware of nothing but the pleasure she was giving me.

I knew I was going to come, the tension was incredible, I tried to hold on for as long as possible but I was powerless against the bliss. When it hit me I screamed out as waves of sensation erupted inside me and swept me into rapture. She kept up the rhythm, prolonging my orgasm for several seconds of unbearable sweetness as I trembled beneath her, carried out of this world by her mouth and her fingers and the perfection of our union.

As the waves of orgasm began to subside, I grabbed Aimee's hair and dragged her head up to my face, kissing her on the mouth so I could taste myself on her lips and tongue. Pulling her on to the bed I thrust my fingers inside her again, knowing that she would come very quickly as I began to kiss and bite her breasts and nipples.

This time it was almost brutal, I drove her furiously towards orgasm, ramming my fingers deep inside, stretching her open, fucking her, fuelling our passion with a primal need for release. As her pussy gripped my fist I sank my sharp canine teeth deep into her flesh. The pain tipped the balance and I felt the tremors of orgasm rippling through her. I drank and she came. Her blood was sweetened as her body surrendered to my touch. She was even sweeter than I had dared hope. She relaxed into my embrace and I fed deeply from her, holding her against me, prolonging her pleasure beyond anything a mere mortal could offer her. I drew her very essence into my veins, filling myself with her. I knew she wouldn't even realise what was happening, her surrender was so willing, so total, all she would know was a moment of total peace. Blood is always better than an orgasm to me, but when it tastes of sex and lust and ecstasy there is nothing better. She was my fountain of life and I shared her pleasure.

The hunger was all encompassing and I had no inhibitions about surrendering to my greed. Her sweet viscous lifeblood filled my mouth and ran unchecked over my jaw and onto her once white gown. When I was almost sated she became limp in my arms. I withdrew my hand from her pussy and slowed my feeding, savouring the last course of my meal. Her eyes were glazed and she had a look on her face that was almost transcendent. I had never seen anything more beautiful.

Her pulse was fading and I knew that I had to choose. I could simply drain her or I could make her immortal, my daughter in blood. As soon as the thought crossed my mind I knew that she was far too special to waste and I had to save her.

I sank my fangs into my own wrist, then held it above her mouth as the blood began to ooze from the wound. The blood dripped onto her lip and instinctively she licked it away. I felt her quicken in my arms as her body responded and her tongue snaked across her lips searching for more. Soon her mouth fastened onto my wrist and she fed from me. Again her eyes closed as though in bliss and she sucked as though in a dream, languid and peaceful as I cradled her against me.

I'd have to hunt again after she'd fed. I didn't have the

energy for both of us, but it wouldn't be like this. It would just be a meal. Maybe one of the homeless who'd willingly give their blood in return for a decent meal. Aimee would need to sleep after her embrace and I'd have an hour or two before the sun came up.

I'd be back before she awakened, and then we would hunt together, sharing endless nights of blood and bliss.

In The Company Of Women
by Sadie Wolf

Sitting outside at a café in the sunshine with her girlfriends, a cappuccino and a chocolate chip muffin in front of her, Kate felt happier than she had in months. Her feet ached from three solid hours of shopping, their table surrounded by bags containing their spoils. What could be better than a weekend in Dublin, celebrating Grace's hen weekend with shopping, drinking and dancing while staying in a nice hotel?

Grace looked relaxed and radiant, a million miles away from those super-stressed brides that seem to have permanent PMT in the months leading up to their big day. Grace was known as the ladylike one amongst them- they used to call her Princess Di – and today was no exception: dressed in a pale blue shift dress and matching cardigan, her neat shoulder length blonde hair catching the sunlight, she looked elegant and pretty. She took out a cigarette and lit it, her engagement ring sparkling in the sun, leaning back in her chair as she inhaled.

'I've promised Stephen I'll give up after we're married.' She said apologetically.

'Good for you. Filthy habit, don't know why you do it.' Jo shook her head. She was fiercely anti-smoking and never let anyone get away with a cigarette without a comment from her. Jo was Grace's best friend and the only one of them who was already married. She ran her own business and wasn't afraid of anyone. 'You can't be worried about getting egg on your face' was one of her sayings. She promoted her business at every opportunity, and when she decided, almost overnight, that she wanted to find a man and settle down, she went about it in the same way, shamelessly approaching and pursuing possible candidates until she met Jack. At which point, in a most un- Jo- like fashion she went all googly-eyed and announced simply that he was "The One" and that was that. Five years later they still clearly adored each other. Jo was a jeans-and-T-shirts kind of girl, albeit designer ones. Like she said, she earned her money and she liked to spend it on well-cut clothes that flattered her figure. She looked at her watch.

'Has anyone heard from the others? Aren't they supposed to be meeting us now?'

Grace shrugged.

'It wouldn't surprise me if they're late.'

'Probably trailing round looking for something suitably organic and tasteless for Helen.' Jo said.

'Now now, she's just very health-conscious.' Grace laughed.

'Don't I know it! Honestly, it was like twenty questions with that poor waiter last night. Mind you, it was good for Jools though, meant he had to keep coming back to the table.'

'She did seem to take an instant liking to him, didn't she?' Grace said.

'Couldn't have been more obvious if she'd tried. Anyway, tell us about this Mercedes. Is it true she's a lap dancer?'

'Now Jo, I don't want you to –'

' But *is* she? I'm not going to say anything to her. Anyway, Jools more or less let the cat out of the bag last night so you can blame her.'

'Ok. Yes, it's true. But she's really nice, so I don't want –'

'Yes yes, I get it. So tell us all about it. Where does she do it?'

'Manchester. Less chance of bumping into someone she knows.'

'But how did she get into it?

'I don't know. I suppose she just walked into a club and asked.'

'Ugh. How could she want to do it? All those sweaty old men.'

Grace shrugged.

'Apparently some weekends she makes a thousand pounds, not bad for two nights' work.'

'Really? She doesn't sleep with them does she?'

'No of course not, she's a lap dancer not a prostitute.' Grace sounded irritated.

'So what's she like?'

'She's nice, you'll like her.'

'I bet she's sickeningly pretty with super long legs and–'

'She *is* gorgeous, but don't hold that against her.'

Kate found herself feeling very uncomfortable during the conversation about Mercedes. She had never met anyone like that before and worried about what she would say to her. Would she accidentally say the wrong thing and offend her? She had a picture in her mind of pole dancers as sleek, effortlessly sexy women with endless legs and boundless confidence. Never in a million years could she imagine having that kind of confidence. In comparison she felt stiff and awkward, conscious of her short legs, her shyness …

'Wake up, Kate!' Grace was laughing at her.

'Sorry, I was miles away. So, anyway, tell me about the dress. Have you got a picture?' Kate asked.

'I've got one on my phone. And loads of other ones as well. We tried on some absolutely hilarious ones for a giggle.'

'Meringue just isn't the word for some of them. Jordan and Peter have a lot to answer for. I deleted the ones of me in those things, they were just too hideous.' Jo added.

'Good job I kept mine then, isn't it!' Grace laughed and showed Kate a photo of the two of them dressed in bright pink crystal-encrusted strapless gowns with huge net skirts, laughing their heads off.

Kate felt a pang of jealousy that she hadn't been part of the dress-trying-on-experience; and that as best friend Jo would be the one who was with Grace the morning of the wedding to help her get ready, whereas Kate would be turning up later as just one of the guests. But then those childish thoughts evaporated and were replaced by a warm and mushy glow as Grace said reverentially, 'that's it' and Kate gazed at a photo of Grace looking serene and lovely in a timelessly beautiful, simple floor-length white dress that made her look like Grace Kelly.

'Gorgeous, isn't it? As soon as she put it on, it was so obvious that was it, and we were just about to give up on that shop before we saw it.'

Kate handed Grace's phone back, feeling a lump in her throat.

'So Kate, do you think you and Darren'll get married anytime soon?' Jo asked.

She looked at her empty plate. The truth was that marrying Darren had an air of inevitability that she found

62

stifling. She knew she was lucky; she shuddered at the thought of being 'Out There' like Jools, drifting haplessly from one dodgy boyfriend to the next. It was clearly infinitely preferable to be like Jo or Grace, but somehow something didn't feel quite right.

She shrugged.

'I guess it's bound to happen one day, but I'm not in any hurry.'

Jo looked at her quizzically, then looked away, distracted.

'Here they are, at last. You two, you're always late!

Even as she bought the dress that afternoon, Kate had had misgivings about it, but these had now developed into full-blown nerves. There was no doubt at all that she looked sexy in it, but did she look *too* sexy? She didn't want to go out looking like a prostitute. Darren certainly would not have approved, she felt sure of that. Although, she thought resentfully, it wouldn't have stopped him looking at other girls wearing similar outfits. She took another look in the mirror. Big brown eyes stared anxiously out from under a straight brown fringe, which joined a shiny brown bob. Her dress was a short black halter-neck with a deep v almost to her waist. She'd had to buy a new bra to go with it, which had given her a most impressive cleavage. Fortunately the sun had been kind to her and her bare shoulders and arms were nicely tanned. She had on sheer black tights and black patent leather heels. She slipped on silver bangles and a plain silver choker and took a deep breath. Holding her head up high, she picked up her bag and went to meet the others in the hotel lobby.

Helen looked slim and elegant in a full-length green silk dress and pashmina. Kate felt sure she wouldn't

63

approve of her dress, although she would be far too polite to say so. Jools was wearing a black leather jacket, black mini-skirt and knee-length leather boots. Grace was wearing a floaty white shirtdress and silver sandals and Jo was wearing black trousers and a white shirt.

When she saw Mercedes, her stomach plummeted. She had let her hair down, and it reached almost to her waist, shiny and honey-coloured. She was wearing a gold sequined backless mini-dress and ridiculously high gold heels, and her endless legs were bare and golden brown.

Kate hadn't yet said more than a few words to Mercedes, as she had arrived later in the afternoon, but now, outside waiting for a taxi, she found herself standing beside her. She could feel Mercedes' eyes on her, like a cat.

'You look great in that dress, it really suits you.'

'Thank you.' Kate blushed. 'You look amazing. That dress is lovely.'

Mercedes smiled.

Five hours later they were in a club called Club M. Helen had gone back to the hotel, professing that she was "too old" for nightclubs; Jools had met a man at the last bar and disappeared. Grace and Jo were dancing in the main arena, and Mercedes and Kate were sitting side by side on a comfy leather sofa in one of the chill-out areas downstairs, sipping vodka and lemonade and people-watching. All night Mercedes had had them in stitches with her unflinching analysis of the male clubbers. They had stood in the gallery looking down at the main arena, Mercedes pointing out men as married, gay, losers or sometimes all three. She brushed off any men who approached her as if they were fruit flies, making Kate giggle with comments afterwards, such as, he's got no money, he's wearing a thirty pound shirt! He's married, no, no ring, I can just tell by the guilty look on his face!

Mercedes' hair smelt of perfume, and her endless legs were stretched out in front of her. Kate thought she was simply the most beautiful woman she had ever seen. Mercedes turned to face her, catching her looking. Kate blushed and looked away. Mercedes reached out her hand and with the lightest of touches brushed Kate's hair away from her face.

'You know, you really are very, very pretty, you know.' Mercedes said, looking straight into her eyes.

There was a pause, and then Kate felt her hand being wrapped in long soft fingers, and Mercedes' hair against her shoulder as she leaned towards her, and then Mercedes' lips were against hers, kissing her. Kate was aware of the softness, the sweetness, how gentle and small she was compared to a man; how lovely it felt to be kissed by women's lips and to have soft long hair against her shoulders.

They ran up the stairs of the hotel holding hands, not noticing or caring if anyone was watching. Mercedes practically pushed Kate through the door of her hotel room, pulling her onto the bed.

It was like music running through and through her, the feel of Mercedes' fingers in her hair, her wet kisses on her mouth. She fiddled with Kate's earrings, trying to undo them, getting them caught up in her hair, giggling, before finally getting rid of them. Mercedes found the zip to Kate's dress, slipping it off to reveal Kate's big breasts spilling out of a black halter-neck bra. Kate sat on the edge of the bed, waiting, and Mercedes smiled at her, then pulled her own dress up and off in a second. She wasn't wearing a bra, only a peach coloured thong.

Mercedes stood in front of her, her long shiny hair reaching down to her small, pointed breasts, a faint tan line visible at the edges of her pale breasts, her stomach tanned and flat. Kate's head span, her stomach contracted. She felt heavy, unable to move, with no idea of what to do next. But then Mercedes saved her, taking Kate's hands in hers, then kneeling down beside her on the carpet, resting her head for a moment on Kate's thigh. Mercedes lifted her head and Kate felt her hair tickling her leg, and then Mercedes kissed her stomach, light, fluttery kisses which made her dizzy, as if she was covered in butterflies as well as full of them.

With one swift movement Mercedes let go of Kate's hands and parted her legs, positioning herself between her knees. The kisses on her stomach continued, only now Kate had her hands free, and tentatively they found Mercedes' shoulders and hair, feeling the movement under her hands, the bones and muscles of her arms, stroking her hair.

Mercedes' hands rested on the bed, then slipped around Kate's waist, pulling her close towards her as she pressed her mouth against her, kissing her firmly now, sucking the tender skin of her stomach, then travelling down to her bikini line, and finally nuzzling against her knickers. Kate could feel Mercedes' hot breath through the fabric, as she deliberately blew onto her knickers, creating a lovely warmth that made Kate immediately wet.

Kate wanted to grab great chunks of Mercedes' hair, to dig her fingernails into her shoulders and arms, but she held herself in, controlled herself, and gently, very gently stroked Mercedes' hair, wound it slowly around her fingers, traced the muscles of Mercedes' arms from her shoulders to her forearms with the lightest of touches. Somehow, she kept herself steady as Mercedes continued her maddening blowing between her legs, which was harder now, and right above her clit.

Kate could feel her clit begin to enlarge and stand out, and then Mercedes began nibbling at it; and Kate couldn't help it, she moaned out loud, and Mercedes seemed to let herself go too. With a swift tug she pulled down Kate's knickers, pushed open her legs and buried her face in her pussy. Mercedes' tongue was everywhere, and her fingers worked inside her, opening her up and pushing hard inside her, finger fucking her hard and fast. While her tongue lapped steadily at her clit, she held her lips open with her fingers, so that she could dip down and lick inside her, lapping up her juices as soon as they appeared.

Kate felt as if her thoughts were being spoken out loud. In her head, she willed Mercedes to finger her harder, to bury her head hard between her legs, to hold her tight, to make her come … And then it felt like all the thoughts in her head exploded as she shook and came against Mercedes' mouth. She clung to Mercedes' shoulders like a helpless child, feeling the shaking spread throughout her body.

Mercedes squeezed her thigh affectionately and stood up, pausing to kiss Kate's stomach and breasts with her wet mouth, and Kate could feel her wet kisses drying on her skin. Mercedes lowered Kate down onto the bed, wrapping her in her arms. Kate lay motionless in Mercedes' arms, dizzy and drunk, every inch of her body tingling and glowing, her heart thudding.

Mercedes' body felt cool and soft in comparison to her own hot afterglow. Kate opened her eyes and saw Mercedes looking at her. There was silence between them, and Kate looked away, feeling shy and awkward once more. Then slowly, almost imperceptibly, Mercedes stretched out her long fingers and gave Kate's nipples the slightest of flicks. They looked at each other and laughed, the tension broken. As Kate relaxed, Mercedes twirled her middle fingers around Kate's nipples, and Kate watched as they quickly stiffened under Mercedes' beautifully manicured fingertips.

Curiosity overcoming shyness at last, Kate reached out and touched Mercedes' pretty little breasts. She had never touched another woman's breasts before, had barely even handled her own. They felt delicate and exquisitely soft, like softened balloons, light and hollow, deliciously smooth and squishy. Kate kneaded them, stroked them and rubbed them, rolling the nipples under the palm of her hand, feeling the heat of the friction and Mercedes' nipples hardening under her hands. She closed her fingertips on the nipples and squeezed; they got harder, she rolled them between her thumb and forefinger, and they got harder still. She experimented – rolling harder, squeezing, increasing the pressure until she was pinching Mercedes' nipples painfully hard.

The little pink nipples were like stones in her fingers, and Mercedes let out a little moan and bent her head, took Kate in her arms and kissed her, deep longing kisses with her tongue right inside her mouth, her lips pressed hard against Kate's lips, Kate feeling the wetness pressed against her, tasting the spicy, musky taste of her pussy in Mercedes' mouth.

Kate's hands were crushed painfully between their bodies, against their breasts, so it was nice when Mercedes shifted position and took hold of Kate's wrist, pushing her hand down. Kate hesitated, for just a moment, but Mercedes kissed her again, gave a longing little moan and opened her legs, pushing herself towards Kate's hand.

Kate moved her hand with more confidence than she

felt. Cupping Mercedes with the flat of her hand she pressed, up and down, circling, hoping that her fingertips would find their way around. Guided by the wetness, her fingers slipped inside the groove and then further, finding the hole.

Even though it was wet and Mercedes was pushing herself up towards her, Kate was still scared of pushing too hard, of hurting her. She slipped her fingers in one at a time, gently and slowly, until Mercedes wouldn't allow it, and, bucking and pushing, encouraged Kate to push harder, to be what felt like being rough to her.

Letting her fingers trail upwards, dragging the wetness with them, she found what she was looking for. Mercedes' clit was a sweet, hard little button that Kate couldn't miss, and as she traced her soaking fingers over it, covering it in wetness, careful not to bruise it, Mercedes moaned and cried out, and pressed Kate's free hand against her breast.

Kate understood, and resumed her squeezing and pinching of Mercedes' nipples. Mercedes found her mouth and kissed her wildly, then fell back onto the pillow and lay with her eyes half closed, as if in a trance, whilst Kate felt masterful and confident.

She knew what she was doing now and she took charge: she pinched Mercedes' nipples harder than she had before, causing Mercedes to cry out, and she held the pinch firm as she got into a rhythm between her legs-pushing her fingers hard into Mercedes' cunt, then trailing her sodden fingers up and over her clit, then down again, all the while keeping a pressure on Mercedes' clit with the heel of her hand as her fingers pushed down inside her. Mercedes bucked, gasping, moaning, clinging to her, then crying out as she came against Kate's hand.

Mercedes lay against Kate's breasts while Kate stroked her hair, feeling Mercedes' pounding heart gradually subside with her breathing.

In the cool air of Mercedes' hotel room, Kate's thoughts were racing. She had never felt so wide-awake. She looked down at Mercedes' tousled brown and golden hair, her long slim body beside her, her pretty nails resting on Kate's arm. Did this mean she was a lesbian? What about Darren? What on earth would the others say? How were they going to explain her sleeping in Mercedes' room?

Mercedes stirred, stretching herself slightly before curling up again against her. The room smelt of sex, shampoo and perfume. She could see the golden glow of the streetlights outside the hotel, their light filtering through the yellow curtains, casting the room in a golden light. Faint sounds travelled up from the street below, but inside the room all was silence, except for the soft sound of Mercedes' breathing.

She had come in Mercedes' mouth! She could still taste herself. And then she had touched Mercedes until she had come. The scent of Mercedes' pussy was on her fingers. It was no good pretending that what had happened had been some kind of aberration, or that she felt at all ashamed. What had happened had shocked her, but she didn't regret it for a second.

The next morning, Kate kissed Mercedes goodbye and, wearing last night's dress she gingerly opened the door. Her own room was at the other end of the corridor. She checked that the coast was clear before making her move, heading down the corridor as fast as she could without actually running, feeling exactly like a naughty schoolgirl. She put her card in the slot and felt the door click, feeling immense relief.

"Kate?"

Jo was standing in the corridor behind her, dressed and looking ready to go.

"Oh, er, hi Jo, I've, er, just got to have a shower. I'll, er, see you in a bit."

Kate closed the door behind her, her cheeks burning. Jo had simply raised her eyebrows at her, but she was not stupid. She really was going to have a shower, and then there was only just going to be time to pack before check-out. Too bad she had missed breakfast, but she could get something at the airport.

One hour later they were gathered in the lobby. A taxi was waiting to take Kate, Jo and Grace to the airport. Mercedes, Jools and Helen were getting a later flight. Kate could feel Jo's eyes on her, but she didn't care. She went up to Mercedes, who was looking naturally gorgeous in a white vest and jeans, and swapped phone numbers, aware that everyone else was watching.

"Taxi!" The cab driver put his head round the door, impatient.

"See you soon, sweetie," Mercedes breathed in her ear, before giving her a hug and a kiss on the lips that was rather more than friendly.

Her face burning, but her heart happy, Kate grinned at the grumpy taxi driver and headed out the door, feeling the curious looks of the others practically boring holes in her back. Seated in the cab, next to a puzzled-looking Grace, Kate looked out and waved, gazing at Mercedes' beautiful hair shining in the sun as she blew Kate a kiss.

The Choice
by Alex Jordaine

Lauren and Sam had been best friends since they'd been pupils at the exclusive school for girls, Roedean, on the East Sussex coast. Sam was lively and outgoing, confident, shrewd, witty and highly creative. She was also a natural beauty, with creamy alabaster skin, feline cheeks, big pale blue eyes, and shoulder-length blonde hair. And, if that weren't enough, she had a figure to die for as well. She was as statuesque as a dancer, an exotic one.

Like Lauren, Sam had been born into money and, like her too, she wore her wealth with consummate ease. This was in no small part because, like Lauren in this respect as well, she was not one of those ladies who lunch. Lauren was doing very well in the publishing field, loved her job. Likewise Sam was making – had made – her mark on the world in her own right and was a very talented and successful fashion designer. The name of Samantha Burrell was now spoken of in the same breath as the likes of Stella McCartney, Alice Temperley and Roland Mouret.

Sam was also unashamedly gay. When asked a very pointed question about her sexuality once by a fashion journalist her reply, repeated with monotonous regularity in the media ever after, had been typically sardonic. 'Put it this way,' she'd said. 'I'm not interested in anything with a tassel.'

It hadn't always been so. She'd had plenty of boyfriends when she and Lauren had been younger; 'boy mad' their parents had said they were in their teens. Lauren had been surprised when Sam had come out as a lesbian. It had been shortly after her own marriage to Mark and she'd wondered illogically if it had something to do with her being in the fashion industry. It seemed to Lauren that it was virtually a statutory requirement for the men in the world of fashion to be gay. Was it perhaps the same with the women?

No, that didn't make any sense at all. Sophie Dahl wasn't gay, nor was Naomi Campbell. Kate Moss wasn't gay either. But hadn't Lauren read somewhere that Kate had enjoyed some dalliances with her own sex, threesomes and the like? Maybe it had begun like that with Sam, starting as a bit of experimentation and ending with her conclusion that she 'wasn't interested in anything with a tassel'. No matter, if Sam was gay, she was gay. It didn't affect their friendship at all. But that, of course, is exactly what it ended up doing.

On the day it all started Lauren had been driving round the centre of London. She was stuck in a slow conga of seemingly interminable traffic, as she tried to find a parking space. When she finally succeeded it happened to be only a stone's throw away from where Sam lived and she decided on a whim to see if she was in. If she was, she thought, perhaps she'd like to join her in what she'd originally been intending to do on her own: have a bit of a shopping spree. She was feeling rather low and thought it might lift her spirits.

Once she'd parked the car and fed the meter, Lauren

walked past a hotel and a short terrace of up-market shops to Palling Court. She arrived at the tall red-brick apartment block, where her friend had lived for the last three years. Sam had always said she wanted to be 'where it was at', right at the heart of things in London. She'd found that with Palling Court, which was in the middle of the West End.

It was an overcast day, the sky the colour of a fogged negative, and there was a damp feeling in the air. There was just starting to be a spatter of rain as Lauren approached the block. Shit, she thought. I haven't brought an umbrella. Perhaps I can borrow one from Sam – if she's in, of course. She pressed the number of her address on the door entry system and hoped for the best.

'Hello,' she heard Sam say.

'It's me, Lauren.'

'Great,' came the friendly response. 'Come on up.'

There was a sharp buzz and Lauren pushed open the front door of the block and made for the lift area. She entered the lift and stared at the wan reflection of her face in the lift's smoked-glass mirror. She decided to put on a brave face for Sam. There was no need to burden her friend with her marital troubles. She emerged from the lift on the tenth floor a few moments later and walked down the spotlessly clean corridor. She stopped outside number 53, where she pressed the bell.

After a few seconds the door was opened by Sam. Lauren thought she looked even more stunning than usual, not least because of what she had on. Her shining blonde hair hung down over the shoulders of an absolute killer dress. It was a clinging little black number with spaghetti straps. Her breasts were almost falling out of its top and it was so short that it barely covered her sex.

She was bare footed and, if Lauren knew her friend,

bare-arsed under that dress, which she guessed might well be one of her own designs. Yes, she looked stunning. She smelled stunning too, some very classy perfume Lauren thought she recognised. It was musky, sexy.

'That's a nice dress you're nearly wearing,' Lauren joked, rolling her eyes.

Sam put her hands on her hips and smiled at her. 'And hello to you too,' she said. 'To what do I owe this honour?'

'I was in the area,' Lauren said. 'I thought I'd try you on the off chance. I hope I haven't caught you at an inconvenient time.'

'Not at all,' Sam assured her. 'Actually, I've just this minute made some coffee. Want some?'

'Sure, thanks.'

Lauren followed Sam down a longish corridor in the direction of the kitchen and allowed her eyes to linger on the sway of her friend's hips, the way her hem kept riding up her naked thigh. She suddenly felt horny. That was funny, she thought. Sam had never had that effect on her before, no girl had. She was straight, not even a bit bi, right. *Right?* Perhaps it was just the effect of that killer dress. Looking at her friend in it was making her mouth dry. She felt she needed that coffee.

'Did you design your dress?' she asked, taking Sam's arm.

'Un huh.'

'What look were you going for?'

'Haute couture meets trailer trash,' Sam replied giving her a sideways look, her eyes shining with mirth.

'You succeeded,' Lauren laughed.

Sam grabbed a couple of mugs when they got to the kitchen and they sat down at the table opposite one another. Sam poured them both coffees from the glass pot on the table and added milk from the jug next to it. They drank quietly for a few moments before Lauren asked, 'So, how are things with you?'

'Very good,' Sam said, taking a sip of coffee. 'Give it another year or two and I'm confident of being bought out by Versace or Dior or one of the other heavy hitters in the fashion business.'

'And you want to be bought out like that, presumably,' Lauren said.

'Oh yes,' Sam replied. 'That way I'll get backing, advertising, money for my shows, accessories, support, it'll be great. It will mean that I'll be able to do the stuff I like doing, and offload what I don't. And it will mean I'll get more time to spend doing other things outside the fashion industry, like spending time with friends like you.'

'That sounds marvellous,' Lauren said. 'I hope it works out for you.'

'Well, there's a way to go but everything seems to be proceeding according to plan so far,' Sam said. 'And it's a goal worth going for. After all, there's more to life than work.'

'God, I wish Mark could get himself a deal like the one you're aiming at,' Lauren said with feeling. Whether Mark wished that himself was quite another matter. Lauren was coming increasingly to the view that her husband preferred spending time at his high-flying job in the big London-based marketing agency of Simpson and Gray to being with her. He desperately wanted a place on the company's board of directors and was working so hard towards that end that it had completely killed his libido. That's what he told her anyway. In any event, he couldn't get it up these days and they hadn't had sex in months.

Sam took a swallow of her coffee. 'He's really busy, is he?' she asked.

'And how,' Lauren said. 'I work hard at my job and really enjoy it but, like you, I think there are limits. You've got to have a life too. The hours Mark has to put in these days are ridiculous. I've barely seen him these last few months. It's like he's married to Simpson and fucking Gray rather than me. I try to be philosophical about it, though. He's so exceptionally busy at present because he's working on a big project that could well mean a major promotion for him, get him onto the board of directors, no less.'

'It can't go on for ever then,' Sam said and Lauren shrugged in a noncommittal way. 'Any end in sight?' Sam persisted, parting her lips quizzically.

'Nope,' Lauren said. 'Well, not at the moment anyway. To tell you the truth, Sam, it's really starting to get me down.' She hadn't meant to say that, had meant to keep her own counsel, keep her matrimonial problems to herself.

'I can see that,' Sam said. 'I thought you were looking pretty stressed out as soon as I saw you, Lauren. Your little joke about my dress didn't fool me, I know you too well.'

'You're a good friend,' Lauren said softly. 'The best.' She drank some more coffee and then put her mug on the table.

The two women were quiet for a time, neither talking nor drinking. Then Sam lifted her mug and took a long sip of coffee. After that she rested her mug on the table and stared at Lauren for several long seconds, frowning. Finally she said, 'I know what you need.'

'A bit of retail therapy,' Lauren said, brightening

slightly.

'Wrong,' Sam replied, with a shake of the head.

'What *do* I need then, wise one?' Lauren asked with a slightly forced smile.

'One of my massages,' Sam said, not skipping a beat. 'It'll do you the world of good, believe me, untense all those muscles. You'll leave this apartment a different woman.' Lauren would remember those words.

'A massage, huh. Do you do "relief"?' Lauren joked, doing the quotation marks in the air thing with her fingers.

'Why?' Sam countered. 'Do you feel in need of relief?' She smiled and looked at Lauren, her pale blue eyes engaging with hers for just a fraction longer than was necessary.

'Don't ask,' Lauren chuckled. Mark might not want sex these days but she sure as hell did and she was feeling thoroughly deprived. She hadn't had sex for ages and ages. Mark wouldn't even deign to give her a pity fuck. But no, that wasn't fair. It wasn't his fault he couldn't get it up, poor guy. Anyway, the point was it had been three whole months since he'd so much as laid a finger on her, and she was a very highly sexed woman with, well, *needs*, for crissake. She felt a twinge of frustrated desire inside her sex, by no means the first she'd felt over the last twelve weeks.

'Come on,' Sam said, getting to her feet. 'Let's be having you.'

Lauren quickly finished the remains of her coffee, set the mug on the table and followed Lauren to her bedroom.

Like the rest of Sam's apartment it was neat and tidy and furnished in a minimalist style. There were low bedside tables either side of the neatly made double bed and at its foot was a wardrobe with well-finished louvered doors. Against the wall beside that was a high-backed chair. There was a chest of drawers with an uncluttered surface up against another wall.

'Off with those clothes,' Sam said in a tone of theatrical command.

'Yes, Miss Dynamic,' Lauren said with a laugh that she was conscious was a little too loud. She undressed, folding her dress over the back of the chair and lining her shoes together under it. She squirmed out of her thong. 'I wasn't flying commando like I bet you are,' she said, giving her friend a grin.

'You're not wrong there,' Sam said with a straight face.

'Shameless,' Lauren laughed.

Sam narrowed her eyes and smiled to suggest that maybe she was right in that assessment. She didn't say anything though. Instead she stopped and stared for a moment, in appreciation, at Lauren's naked form.

'Who are you staring at, mate?' Lauren said mock-aggressively in a ridiculous 'mockney' accent.

Sam raised an amused eyebrow at Lauren's impersonation. 'I love your figure,' she said, letting her eyes sweep over Lauren's body once more. 'It's so shapely, such a refreshing change from all the stick insects I work with all the time in my trade.'

'You're not so bad yourself,' Lauren replied, tilting her head back a little and lowering her eyelids, letting her gaze go up and down that floaty-clingy-sexy dress, appraise that lovely figure, those beautiful unbound breasts, those shapely thighs.

Sam gave her more than an appraising look as she did this, which did not go unnoticed by Lauren. She wants me, Lauren found herself thinking. I never realised that before. And I want her. I *certainly* never realised that before. She could imagine tonguing her friend's pussy, could imagine putting her fingers inside her. She was getting not a little turned on and could tell that behind the impassive, slightly amused expression that Sam was wearing she was turned on too.

'Get onto the bed and roll over onto your front,' Sam said, ostensibly all business. 'I'm going to knead your back from neck to ankles. You'll really feel the benefit.'

Lauren lay on her stomach on top of the bedspread and her hair fell loosely across her face. She tucked her arms under one of the pillows, leaving the swell of her breasts visible where they pressed against the mattress. Her back sloped downward to the valley at the base of her spine, and then rose again at the graceful curve of her glorious backside.

True to her word, Sam started at the top, touching the back of her neck. From there she moved across her shoulders, kneading the muscles there. It felt great, really relaxing, and Lauren gave herself to the experience. Next Sam began stroking gently down the top of her spine and over her shoulder blades, gliding her hand gently over her skin.

Then she planted a small kiss on Lauren's neck. 'It's so lovely to see you,' she said softly. 'You're adorable.' Lauren gave a little shudder in response. She could feel herself go wet between the legs.

Sam massaged her back some more – a kind of soft pummelling, awakening the skin, warming the muscles. 'Mmm,' Lauren said. 'You're so good at this.'

Sam moved down to her feet then and began to softly caress her calves, stroking them, feeling her slim muscles. Lauren imagined her friend kissing and licking her calves, each of her toes, worshipping her feet. The thought of it created an ache between her legs and her clit began to twitch.

Then Sam knelt on the bed and moved up her thighs. 'Your skin is so soft here,' she purred. The ache between Lauren's legs was getting more acute. Her pussy felt slippery. Sam pushed Lauren's legs apart to make room for herself and Lauren nearly climaxed there and then. She could feel her blood singing in her veins and her breath was coming quicker. Sam trailed her fingers lightly over her thighs. Lauren was now soaked.

And then it happened. Sam plunged her fingers into all that wetness between Lauren's legs, making her groan with desire. She began pushing her fingers in and out of her pussy fast and hard and, God, it felt *so* good.

Then Sam did something else. She brought her mouth to Lauren's rear cheeks and pressed her lips to her anus, licking her until she trembled with desire. And all the while her tongue was flick-flick-flicking its magic over Lauren's anus she carried on masturbating her, making her clitoris pulse with a moist insistent throb until, all her nerves singing, a powerful orgasm shook and scorched her to ecstasy.

Finally Lauren fell back down to earth. She rolled over then, revealing her naked breasts and erect brown nipples and the copious wetness between her thighs. She brushed her long hair from her face and looked into Sam's eyes. 'Your turn now,' she said.

Sam's eyes were shiny and her breathing shallow as she pulled her dress off, exposing herself entirely to her friend, her lover. Her body was perfect, Lauren thought. She pulled Sam down into her arms and pressed her lips to hers and kissed her hard as she rolled on top of her. Sam kissed her right back and the kiss felt fantastic.

Lauren then put her lips to Sam's throat and licked a

gentle trail down to her sex and began kissing her there. Her pussy was as wet and gleaming as her own and Lauren subjected it to a persistent licking. Sam groaned deeply and ran her hands up over her stiff nipples as Lauren licked deep inside her. She cried out in total abandon when she licked her to a blissful orgasm.

Then Lauren slithered back up the bed and the two women looked at each other. They held the look, their eyes locked, and then they both smiled. No words were necessary. They kissed for a very long time after that, losing themselves in the kiss. Then they lay quietly on their backs, Lauren's arm under Sam's neck, Sam's head on her left shoulder. Their naked bodies were damp from their recent efforts.

'I love you,' Sam said 'I always have, you know. I love everything about you.'

Lauren sighed. 'I love you too,' she said. It was true. She'd always loved Sam as the closest of friends and now they had enjoyed the most incredible sex together as well. What was that but romantic love? Or *was* it just sex? It certainly wasn't any old sex, that was for sure. This was the kind of sex she'd been denied for too long – mind blowing, ecstatic, out of this world. She loved Sam for it. She needed her for it. She ached for it. They made love again. And again. And again, over and over.

It was only when they finally stopped and Sam, all passions spent at last, lay slumbering peacefully by her side, that the guilt began to set in with Lauren. What in God's name was she going to do about Mark, she wondered anxiously. She looked up at the ceiling, her face clouded with concern. One thing was certain, she told herself. She must not tell him about what had happened between her and Sam. It was essential that she keep quiet about that. It would have to be her guilty secret.

And that was what it remained for the next three months as her affair with Sam raged like a forest fire. Finally Sam gave her an ultimatum. She told her: 'It's him or me'. Lauren was fed up with all the deception, all the lies she'd been telling Mark about the non-existent business trips she was going on all the time, the fictitious conference she'd attended in Paris and the other in Milan. Not that he took any real notice of anything she said these days.

Things really were at their lowest ebb between Lauren and her work-obsessed husband. She saw Mark very rarely indeed now and when she did, he just wasn't there. He was present in the flesh, sure, but it was like his mind had travelled to another planet – the planet Simpson and fucking Gray. He was completely and utterly consumed by his work now, by his overwhelming ambition. 'It's him or me,' Sam had said. Lauren made her choice.

Glass Houses
by Heidi Champa

I'm the first one to admit it; I'm a snoop. Every since I can remember, I've always gotten such a thrill from searching out the answers to secrets and surprises. Christmas, birthdays, you name it. I've never been any good at waiting. If there was something I wanted, I wanted it now. But, when that wasn't an option, I always had to satisfy myself and my curiosity. Even now, as a grown woman, I couldn't control the urge to find out what Maggie was hiding from me.

The box was black velvet. The smooth and soft surface felt so good under my fingers. I had found it in the back of the closet, after just a few minutes of snooping. I knew she was hiding something. I knew she was being more sneaky than usual. The lid hinge creaked slightly as I pulled it open. There it was. The most beautiful dildo I had ever seen.

I had seen it first months ago, at the toy store downtown. It was perfect; glass, thick and long, with a red swirl from base to tip. We had been shopping for lingerie when it caught my eye, transfixing me with its shiny beauty. Before we had left the store, I had already begun fantasizing about it slipping into me, strapped to my partner's perfect hips. The smooth surface would ease into me so sweetly. I just had to convince her to buy it for me. Sure, I could have bought it for myself. But thinking about my dear, sweet girl, walking into that shop and bringing that perfect piece of glass home was part of what made it all so hot. It had become such a pervasive fantasy, the glass finally settling between my pussy lips, my Maggie making me beg for more. If only I could make her want it as much as I did.

I had hinted many times about how much I would like to feel that dildo in my pussy. Nothing seemed to entice her enough to buy it. It had clearly become her way of teasing me, making me wait until I couldn't bear it anymore. When I finally gave up, my only consolation became that I would receive it as a gift someday. Obviously, my hints hadn't fallen on deaf ears. We had used toys before, many times. But, for some reason this one had taken a hold of me like no other before it. Now that it was in my hand, I could hardly believe it was finally going to fill my pussy, like it had filled my thoughts.

Maggie never let on that she had purchased the glass cock. It was just as I thought; she was teasing me all this time. I wondered if she enjoyed my begging as much as I did. Usually, she never made me wait for gifts or tokens of her affection. I was somewhat spoiled by her. Not that she minded, most of the time. This was clearly her way of teaching me a lesson; one I was eager to learn. I held the dildo in my hands, feeling it for the first time. I could feel my pussy getting wet, the anticipation getting the better of me. Now all I had to do was wait, for her to give it to me. But, who knew how long that would be?

I didn't hear the front door open. I didn't hear her footfalls on the hardwood. Too caught up in my own fantasy, she surprised me with her voice.

"What are you doing?" She looked at me from the doorway, her arms folded. I was caught. She glanced at the dildo, then back to my blushing face. She walked towards me and sat down. Taking the toy from my hands, she finally looked me in the eyes.

"You were snooping again. How many times have I told you about that?" Her hand slipped down my cheek gently. I looked down at the dildo, sitting in her lap. I worried that she would make me wait even longer for it now.

"I'm sorry. I just couldn't help myself."

"I told you to be patient. But you had to have it now, didn't you? Well, maybe I should give you your wish. That's what you want, isn't it?"

I didn't need to answer. She picked up the dildo and brought its cool surface up to my lips. I tried not to shudder as the glass head smoothed over my mouth, and I couldn't resist sticking my tongue out to taste it. Maggie took this as a chance to push it gently between my lips, being careful not to bang into my teeth.

"Close your eyes, my dear." I did as she wanted, as I always did.

The cool glass quickly started to heat up in my mouth, as I sucked the head of the dildo. I could feel the flush of heat growing between my legs, just having the toy in my mouth. She pushed it deeper, my gentle sucking turning more intense. My eyes remained closed, even though I desperately wanted to see my Maggie. I snuck a peek at her face, her eyes intently watching me. She pulled the dildo from my lips, replacing it with her hot mouth. The kiss, the sweep of her tongue on mine threw more gas on my fire. I let my hands roam over her, settling on the gentle slopes of her breasts. Her nipples swelled under the cotton of her blouse, and I could tell she wasn't wearing a bra.

Maggie took my hand and led me up the stairs. I could hear the glass of the dildo gently clacking against her topaz ring. I sat on the edge of the bed and watched as she opened her blouse slowly, each button more of a production than the last. Her skirt fell to the floor, revealing stockings clinging to her perfect thighs. I moved to stand up, to touch my beloved, but she pushed me back down on the edge of the bed. She opened the drawer next to the bed, and I watched her slip into her beautiful leather harness. I could barely breathe. Coming towards me, I couldn't take my eyes off her beautiful body.

Lifting my arms, she pulled my shirt over my head, her pussy just beyond its leather restraint. I could smell her excitement, as I was sure she could smell mine. She allowed me to stand up long enough to remove my pants, leaving my damp panties exactly where they were. I watched with an unflinching gaze as, pushing me to my knees, she attached the most beautiful toy I had ever seen snugly into the harness.

I reached up to feel her wet sex, the slick wetness sliding under my fingers. As I eased two fingers inside her, she pushed the dildo between my lips again. She rocked her hips against my teasing fingers, as the dildo slid effortlessly into my mouth. Moans escaped her lips as I flicked my thumb over her clit. Maggie made the most exquisite noises when I fingered her. The head of the dildo hit gently against the back of my throat, I followed the red swirl from base to tip with my tongue.

"God, you are so beautiful." Her sweet words filled my ears. I looked up at Maggie, my eyes straining to look at her face.

She pulled me up to my feet, and reached her tiny

hand into my panties. I groaned as I felt her fingers practically melt into my wet flesh. She pushed inside me with almost no effort, my pussy putting up no resistance. I was far too excited. Soon, I was lying back on the bed, my panties taking the long slow trip down my legs to the floor. Her hot mouth was between my legs before I could take another breath. Sweeping her tongue across my clit, she dived inside my cunt with two fingers, thrusting them inside in a slow rhythm. The pad of her thumb came to rest on my tight little button, rubbing circles over and over.

"You want me to fuck you, don't you?" I could barely breathe, let alone think to answer her with words. I nodded, but she wasn't going to let me off the hook that easy. Her mouth attacked my cunt yet again, bringing me closer and closer to the edge. I wanted that toy inside me so badly, but she was going to make me beg; just like I wanted her to.

"I want you to fuck me. Please, Maggie. Please, I need it." My words were tumbling out of my mouth in a torrent. I continued to blather on and on as she knelt on the bed between my legs, rubbing her fingers, moist from my pussy on the dildo's hard surface. Maggie's smooth hand ran down my thigh, sending quivers up to my spine. I saw the glistening tip of the toy come to rest between my swollen pussy lips, and she swirled the cool surface over my weeping gash. Teasing me with slow circles of torturous pleasure, I thrust my hips at her helplessly, as a smile played across her lips.

"You want it so bad, don't you, my dear? I was going to make you wait a while longer, but you just had to go and be a little snoop. I guess I'll just have to make you come with this beautiful cock right now. But promise me you won't snoop any more."

Maggie smiled again. She knew I would never be able to stop snooping. I could make her a thousand promises, but we both knew my resolve would crumble at the very next opportunity. But, at that moment I would have said anything, promised anything, to get her to fuck me.

She was really starting to enjoy herself. The head of the cock eased inside me, spreading me open inch by inch. Just as I was relishing the fullness inside my pussy, she pulled back. I couldn't suppress the whimper of disappointment from escaping my throat.

"God, Maggie. I promise, I promise. Please, I can't take it any more. Fuck me. Fuck me with that amazing cock."

"Promise what? What do you promise?"

"I promise I'll never snoop again. I swear it. I promise I'll never do it again. Please, Maggie. Please. I swear it. I won't snoop ever again."

Her smile spread open wide, and I felt the dildo easing into me, slowly. So slowly. Finally, I felt the leather harness against my bare flesh. She was in me to the hilt. Planting a slow, deep kiss on my lips, Maggie pumped her hips into me, my legs wrapping around her to take every thrust. She moved in and out of me deliberately, each powerful stroke going deeper than the last. The glass had warmed inside me, the rippled surface teasing my cunt from the inside out. The leather harness, so soft and supple, grazed my sensitive clit with each teasing swirl of her hips. I felt the rumble of my orgasm building inside me. Maggie closed her lips around an aching nipple, flicking her hot tongue over it until I couldn't stand any more pleasure. I bucked my hips against her, and felt my orgasm breaking and crashing through me. I shook and writhed beneath her beautiful body, her hands guiding my hips on to the massive dildo, riding me through my ecstasy.

As I returned to earth, the first thing I saw was my beautiful Maggie, her eyes glowing, stroking my hair. I could only manage a small smile, my body weak from coming so hard. I looked down at the beautiful toy, still glistening between her legs. Maggie smiled at me and kissed my lips lightly.

"It's a shame you didn't find your other surprise. I guess you didn't look hard enough. Oh well, I guess you'll just have to wait. Since you promised and all."

She and I both knew I could never last. The punishment for snooping was just too much fun.

Dancing Queen
by Elizabeth Cage

'Happy birthday, Jo. This should give you hours of pleasure.'

'Cheers, Kelly,' I replied, impatiently peeling away the lavender tissue paper. I grinned as it revealed a luminous pink vibrator.

'Thought your old one must be worn out by now,' she joked. 'I've already put the batteries in, so it's ready for use.'

'You know me so well.'

'No time to use it now, you greedy bitch. Later,' she laughed. 'Are you ready? We'll be late, otherwise.'

'Do you think it's too short?' I asked, smoothing down my new leopard-print dress.

'A dress can never be too short,' she proclaimed. 'Bend over.'

I obeyed. Kelly frowned. 'Let's just say I can see what you had for breakfast.'

I smiled. 'Filthy cow. Ready to go, then?'

It was a sultry summer night and even with the car windows open, it felt hot and stuffy as Kelly drove into the packed car park of the Tonic Singles Club. In a way, I suppose, we came here on false pretences. True, we were the prerequisite over thirty. Easily. And we were both unattached. But that isn't why we came. We were not looking for love, as the song goes.

'Evening, girls. Can I see your membership cards?'

Nigel, the doorman, dressed in black dress suit and bow tie, took a pride in doing his job properly, even though we were regulars. As I fumbled in my pouch bag for the plastic membership card, my feet began to tap instinctively as strains of funky commercial house music filtered down from the upstairs room.

'Okay, girls. Have a good evening.'

Our first stop was, of course, the toilets. Pushing past the cubicles, air heavy with a cocktail of hairspray and perfume, I elbowed my way to the mirror to check my make-up while Kelly had a pee.

'Got your pen?' she asked, from behind the door.

'Check.'

'Paper.'

'Check.'

'Right.' The toilet flushed and she emerged, eyes radiant, ready for action.

We made our entrance, strutting through the kaleidoscope of flashing, swirling lights, the thump-thump of the bass sending vibrations through our bodies. It was a guest DJ tonight. As usual, I sauntered over.

'Play any requests?' I asked.

'What do you want?'

I'd already scribbled on a piece of paper. He glanced down. 'What's this? *War and Peace*?' My request list was ten deep. I smiled sweetly.

Kelly got us a table behind the speakers. She gestured across the crowded dance floor. 'You think your dress is short - look at that woman over there, flashing the gash. Hey, he's playing *Booty Luv*. Let's get us some floor space.'

We danced alone and around each other, Kelly swaying, her eyes closed. Savouring the sounds. Absorbing the music. She looked good as always, wearing a red dress, ribbon-thin straps, short, with a scoop neckline. The dress hugged her lithe, toned body, highlighting her slim waist. She moved her bronzed arms above her head.

The rhythm was pounding, pulsating, pumping.

'I'm streaming,' said Kelly, tweaking her waxed spikes of white-blonde hair. Sweat was pouring down her face, dripping down her neck into the crevice between her small neat breasts. 'Back in a mo. Have to cool down.'

As she exited, the tempo changed to the slow wailing of Celine Dion and a man beside me muttered, 'Erection section. It's a groper.'

I pretended to rifle through my bag, avoiding eye contact with any male who might want to slow dance. Or smooch, as we used to call it when I was a teenager. In the days when we went to the church disco and leapt about to the songs of Sweet and T Rex and Mud and the Rubettes. And played strip poker in the shed outside with a group of older kids, boys and girls.

'Not dancing?' I looked up to see a guy with a nervous smile.

I shook my head. 'No thanks, not to this. Too slow for me.'

'Perhaps later?'

'Okay.' He walked away and was soon on the dance floor with a petite redhead in a halter-neck dress, her breasts brushing against his aubergine shirt.

I hoped Kelly wouldn't be much longer. I disliked sitting there alone. I'd known her since school. We just clicked right away. Did everything together. Best friends.

Until she'd married Shaun. After that, we'd drifted apart, although she still phoned occasionally and we met for a drink sometimes. Then, one night about a year ago, to celebrate her divorce, we went to a nightclub together and I remembered how much I'd loved to dance in my teens, how I missed it. I got such a high, such a buzz, that we started to go out together every week.

Kelly finally returned, looking flushed. 'It's too hot,' she complained. 'Slowies still going on?'

'Last one,' I replied. They usually played in sets of three and we were at last on to *Lady In Red*.

'I hate that song,' muttered Kelly. 'I hope he puts some decent music on next.'

Thankfully, one of my requests followed. When I danced to one of my favourite tunes I closed my eyes and I felt like I was having sex in public, it turned me on so much. I loved to play slutty girl.

Afterwards, I was sweating. I wished I could take something off, but resisted when I recalled the time at another club when I wore a cut-off T-shirt over what was quaintly described as a crop top. I'd taken the tee-shirt off. No sooner was it over my head than a bouncer appeared. He'd thought I was undressing.

'You can't do that here.'

'Why not?'

'You can't show your bra.'

'It's not a bra. It's a crop top.'

Brazenly, I'd strode onto the dance floor. I heard a couple of guys muttering that I was a tart and much worse. It hurt my feelings, if the truth be told.

'What's their problem?' I'd said to Kelly later. 'I wasn't hurting anyone.'

'Some people are just prudes. They can't face up to their own sexuality.'

We danced to an R&B set and then some 80s classic dance tracks before going outside for a swig of water.

'Not bad tonight is it?' said Kelly.

'Not bad,' I agreed.

'Hey, isn't that –?'

'– *Naughty Girl*.'

We returned to the floor, moving slowly, sensuously to the sexy beat. In our own space at first. Then Kelly started to move towards me and I knew what would happen next. She danced around me and we were back to back, brushing against each other, hips touching. Then, as the music changed, she turned and we danced opposite, facing each other, inches apart, and I could taste her breath. She bent her knees, legs apart, swaying from her waist, her smooth arms snaking the air. I mirrored her movements, our eyes locked and we became fused together by music and rhythm and a longing so powerful it hurt. People were watching us. I felt them watching, wondering. I loved the fact that they were looking at us. It made me feel hornier than ever.

'What do you think they made of our floorshow?' laughed Kelly, smoothing down her sweat-soaked dress. Like me, she loved the attention. I grinned back at her. But tonight, something was different. Tonight, there was something else between us. I could feel it, like an electric charge. Tonight, I wanted this to be more than just an act. I moved closer to Kelly, and as we swayed, our nipples touched and I felt a warm tingle between my legs. She didn't move away and I wondered if she was feeling what I was feeling. I slipped my hands around her waist, pulling her towards me, our bodies pressed together. I wanted to kiss her.

Then the music stopped. For a moment, we remained locked together. Then, blushing, she said, 'It's so hot in here. I need to get some air.'

'I'll come with you,' I said, following her outside.

Standing beneath the dark, star-studded sky, I noticed she was trembling.

'Is anything wrong?' I asked anxiously.

She shook her head.

'Do you want to go?'

'Maybe.'

We got into her car but she didn't start the engine. It was strange, seeing Kelly, who was usually so in control, suddenly unsure of herself.

'Hey, relax,' I reassured her, stroking her bare arm.

She turned to look at me and I noticed that her eyes were hungry. I leaned across and kissed her on the mouth, gently at first, tentatively, exploring her lips with the tip of my tongue. She didn't resist, and I got the feeling she was considering the sensation. Slowly, she opened her mouth and I pushed my tongue deeper inside. She started to groan softly.

While one hand cradled her head, I let the other hand rest on her right breast, gently kneading her nipple between my thumb and forefinger through the fabric of her dress. Her nipple was already hard, and I felt a thrill of excitement at her response to my touch. Still kissing her, I carefully slipped the thin red straps off her shoulders, sliding the dress down to her waist to reveal her naked breasts. Her eyes were closed and I let my mouth move down to her left breast, caressing her nipple with my tongue, circling and darting, until she was wriggling with pleasure.

'Do you like this, Kelly?' I whispered.

She moaned. I smiled, enjoying this unexpected feeling of power.

She was breathing harder now, so I slid my hand

down between her parted legs.

'God, Kelly, you're so wet,' I exclaimed, pretending to sound shocked.

She wasn't the only one. I started to stroke her, and her moans became louder.

'Shh, someone might hear,' I warned, thinking that people could come out to the busy car park at any moment.

'I don't care,' she breathed, clamping my hand tight. 'Don't stop.'

The smell of her desire was overpowering and I buried my head between her thighs, teasing her clitoris with my tongue.

'You taste so good,' I told her, between lapping at her juices. By now her body was tensing and arching, her cries louder. I continued to lick, to savour her, while my fingers played with her nipples and as she came the first time, I was aware of the music pounding insistently through the open doors of the night-club, where only minutes before we were dancing together.

When she came again, her groans were so loud I had to cover her mouth with mine to stifle her cries. We clung to each other for a while, the sweat from our bodies mingling.

'Do you want to go back inside?' I asked, when her groans had subsided.

'I have a better idea,' she replied thoughtfully. 'Why don't we go back to your place and we can christen your birthday present. Thank goodness I bought heavy duty batteries. We're going to need them.'

Summer Camp
by Eva Hore

This working camp was stupid. I hated it. Why we had to watch sheep being shorn, bulls being lassoed and cows milked was beyond me. It was a ridiculous waste of time.

While everyone was focused on the activities I decided to sneak down to the barn, smoke a joint and relax. Lying on the soft straw was as close to nature as I wanted to get.

'And what do you think you're doing?' a voice in the stall next to where I was lying spoke.

'I … er …' I wasn't sure what to say. Didn't know who it was.

'You'd get into so much trouble if I told anyone you were smoking down here. One spark and this whole barn would go up.'

It was one of the owner's daughters. She looked butch and she was eyeing me like she was interested. I thought I'd bait her, see how far she'd go.

'Well maybe you should punish me then,' I said smugly.

'You know I think I'll do just that. Get over here.'

With the cigarette dangling from my lips I sauntered over. Snatching it out of my mouth, she drew on it before extinguishing it in a bucket of water and then grabbed me

98

by the arm.

'Get in there,' she said, pointing to someone's quarters.

As she slammed the door shut I took a quick look around. The room was neat and sparsely furnished. A chair, single bed, small table and a cupboard. I tried not to giggle as I looked back at her.

'You think this is funny, do you?' she asked.

'Well … yeah,' I muttered.

'Take your clothes off,' she ordered.

'What?' I hadn't counted on her being so forward, so keen.

'I said take your clothes off and do it now,' she said picking up a small riding crop that was hanging on the wall. I quickly did as she asked as she slapped the whip into the palm of her hand.

I was excited as I stood there proudly in front of her showing her she couldn't intimidate me.

'Now sit on that chair,' she said.

'What about I just lie on the bed,' I said coyly. Being stark naked in front of a stranger was such a turn on. I wondered what she thought about my body, how it would feel with her hands touching me.

'I said sit on the chair. Now,' she said menacingly.

I sat, the cold wood causing goosebumps to appear on my skin.

'Put your hands behind your back,' she said giving me a quick slap to the thigh with the whip when I took too long to comply.

The stinging pain shot through me as though zapped by lightening. My pussy began to throb and my nipples hardened. Holding my hands together she lashed rope to them and then secured me to the back of the chair. I was breathing heavily – turned on like never before. She stood behind me, her hands grabbing at my breasts and pinching the flesh cruelly. She pinched the nipples, pulling them hard until I cried out.

'Quiet,' she demanded. 'I don't want to have to explain why I'm doing this to you if someone walks in.'

Standing in front of me she licked her lips as she placed the whip hard up against my neck, before holding it to my lips.

'Lick it,' she said.

I opened my mouth and licked the leather staring up at her.

'Very good,' she said.

Taking the whip she trailed it down over my breasts, rubbed it against my nipples, the rough straps of leather caressing my skin. My arms strained against the rope causing my breasts to jut forward, making me very aware of how vulnerable I was and wondering what she would do next.

She flicked the whip against my heaving breasts and I moaned with pleasure as the leather tantalised my fevered skin. She began to slap my torso with it, my shoulders, my waist, my thighs. I could feel my pussy throbbing against the wooden chair and knew my juices would be wetting the seat.

As she knocked my thighs apart with the whip, I sat there desperately wishing she would touch me. Instead she demanded I open my legs wider.

'Put them up on the railings on the side of the chair, you stupid girl,' she said.

As I did that I became very focused on my pussy. It too was jutting forward, begging to be touched. She walked around me, grabbed an ankle and tied it to the chair. Then she tied the other one. Now I was completely at her mercy.

She ran the handle down over my slit and then back up again. I moaned wanting desperately for her to do it again. My clit was throbbing as she rubbed harder.

'You like that don't you?' she whispered.

'Oh yeah,' I said.

'What if I push the handle in further, like this. Do you like that too?'

'Oh yeah, that's beautiful. Keep going,' I begged on the verge of coming.

'I give the orders,' she said stopping immediately.

There was a clothes hoist folded up behind the cupboard. She partially dragged it out and pulled two clothes pegs off it. With a glint in her eye and a smirk on her lips she strode back to me and without warning attached them to my nipples.

I nearly screamed out but a quick flick on my thigh telling me to be quiet had me perspiring and anxious from pain. Placing her fingertips on the ends of the pegs she slowly squeezed down making the pain nearly unbearable.

'Quiet,' she hissed as noise came from my throat. 'You like being punished don't you?'

'Yes,' I whispered, pain causing my eyes to squeeze tightly shut.

'Open your eyes,' she demanded, 'and keep them open.'

With every breath I took the pegs burned into my nipples. I watched as she stripped out of her clothes. I was eager to see her nude, to have her body pressed up against mine, our pussies touching.

She had small breasts, her nipples dark and inviting and a thick patch of pubic hair covered the triangle between her thighs. My body pulsed with desire and my nipples screamed with pain as they hardened under the

101

pegs.

She straddled me, her pussy nearly touching mine as she thrust a breast into my mouth. I sucked on it greedily as she ground herself further down on my lap. She held my head with her hands, smothering me as she rubbed her tits across my face. My tongue flickered out, eager to taste her, wanting to suck more, suck harder.

Her hand slipped between our bodies and her fingers slid down over my throbbing clit. I gasped with pleasure wanting nothing more than for her to finger me, to sink her fingers deep inside my cunt and explore me before finger fucking me.

But she didn't.

Dropping down further so her arse was nearly touching the seat of the chair she looked down at our pussies and then back up at me. She rocked back and forward our pussy lips just grazing each others. I was panting with desire as her palm stole down and rubbed against my wet lips.

She pushed her chest back into me, the pegs rubbing against my nipples while her mouth tantalised my face, kissing my forehead and my cheeks before her tongue licked lazily over my top lip. I opened my mouth to receive her kiss but she pulled back, laughing as she teased me.

Then she was off and behind me. Grabbing the chair she lowered it on the floor so my back was flat on the ground and my head resting at her feet. I could see straight up into her cunt and watched fascinated as she spread her legs and slowly lowered herself down to my mouth.

My tongue stretched forward desperate to taste her. Her scent wafted over me, enveloping me as her pussy lips grazed my face, before rubbing her slit over my nose to part her lips.

I moved my head and she slapped my thigh. 'Not until I'm ready,' she said.

I lay there as she straddled my face, suffocating me with the weight of her body. She tasted musky, sweet and tangy. I lapped greedily at her pussy, sucking on her lips, trying desperately to latch on to her clit as her juices oozed out of her.

'Oh yes,' I mumbled into her pussy as her fingers parted my own lips and slipped inside me. First one finger, then two, then more. She smeared my juices over me, wetting my clit, smearing them down the inside of my thighs before pulling back the hood over my clit and rubbing madly.

I sucked her harder, my tongue flickering around, trying to please her like she was pleasing me. Then something hard was probing me and I knew she'd inserted the handle of the whip, knew that finally she was going to fuck me with it and I came, came all over it when suddenly we both froze.

We heard voices in the stables. She rose leaving me lying there helpless as she opened the door a crack and peered out. Shutting the door she quickly pulled on her clothes, straightened herself up and made to leave.

'Hey,' I hissed. 'Where are you going?'

'Back to work,' she said opening the door wide.

I hoped no one was there. Imagine what someone would think, me lying naked on a chair on the floor with pegs still attached to my nipples. My pussy throbbed and my body pulsated not only with fear but excitement too. She laughed and came back to me. Righted the chair and untied me.

As I dressed she left the room, turning at the door to smile at me, 'Be back here tonight at nine and we'll finish what we started and if you're good I might just tie you up on the block and tackle we have out here in the shed,' she said and then was gone.

I hurried back to the others, my pussy saturated, my nipples aching eager for the day to finish and the night to begin.

Losing It
by Ashley Hind

I remember it being the hottest day of a warm summer, and somewhere amongst the manic urgency and dripping need of that afternoon, she took something from me I never thought I'd lose. Sometimes I think it was all a dream; the events had that surreal ease that only ever happens in films or fantasy. But now when I close my eyes and fuck my wet hole with the same slapping abandon that started it all, I can still feel her behind me, her hands gripping my thighs, and the delicious slide that opened me up and shot me through with a pain that melted into ecstasy, and made me come harder than I'd ever come before.

I hadn't even known she was in, or I wouldn't have been caught in the first place. The house was quiet and I had got up late after a too-boozy evening with my cousin, Mandy. Every year since her divorce she has come to stay for a couple of weeks over the summer holidays. She lives in the Somerset sticks, in a village so remote you expect her to cower in the face of modern technology such as petrol-driven transport and electricity. Due to our proximity to London, coming here gives her a cheap break, and a way of alleviating the monotony that their imposed village exile brings, particularly to her daughter,

Emma.

My husband doesn't mind the invasion, probably because he has always fancied Mandy-With-The-Big-Tits, and she in turn is a relentless flirt. Emma is now in her final school year, and connected to the world of "cool" by the internet and her mobile phone- when she can get a signal, of course. That doesn't stop my daughter, although she is a couple of years younger, relishing her role as sophisticated urbanite host, and bringer of all things amazing to her country cousin. But Emma was about to grow up, and she and I were going to stumble into something that neither of us expected.

I love to wank, and I love to get carried away by my filthy thoughts and the sometimes insatiable needs of my body. I can be immersed in desire for hours, incapable of suppressing the rude daydreams that can have me reaching for my vibrator several times before my husband comes home to fill and sate me. That morning, I was fantasising about Mandy forcing me into submission, smothering me with her pillow chest and then sitting on my face.

As usual, I was lying on my back diagonally across the bed, and had whipped myself into a frenzy with the vibrator alone. As my orgasm approached, I lifted my legs right up and raised my head to get a view in the cheval mirror as I plunged my fingers as deeply as possible into my hot cunt and fucked myself hard and fast. I pictured my hand as Mandy's, a saturated, pumping blur at my wanton snatch. And that's when I saw her, a background reflection as transfixed at the sight in the mirror as I was.

Even when my mind had processed the information and told me that young Emma was watching my rude and noisy act, I still couldn't stop myself. I was just too close to the finish. I always kept my bedroom door partially open for early-warning signs from downstairs of unexpected returns. Although outside the room and obscured from direct vision, Emma could see me in all my wanking glory, as clear as day in the mirror. And I could see her, mouth open and with breaths coming fast, one hand down between her thighs and clutching her crotch through her cut-down jeans.

The sight of her lost in obvious rapture sent me towards my climax. It built with unstoppable energy, and just before it broke, my gaze lifted from her squeezing hand, up over the small swell of her breasts beneath her T-shirt, and upwards to her pretty face. For an instant our eyes met in the mirror, but the power of my release forced mine shut and sent my body shaking as I bucked against my sodden fingers and wanked the flow from inside me as the vibrator buzzed at my clit. By the time I was able to open my eyes again, she was gone.

I expected her to avoid me all day, but she was downstairs quietly eating toast when I pulled myself together and went down for breakfast. She was cheery and acted as if nothing had happened, doing her level best to make easy conversation and avoid any embarrassing silences and therefore the need for apologies or explanation. In return, I tried to push from my mind the memory of her hand between her legs, and the recurring visions of her alone and naked, her legs up and wide open, mirroring my dirty actions.

She told me she hadn't spent another day sight-seeing with her mum and my daughter as she wanted to go into town to get a dress for her sixth-form prom night. She was hoping that I would take her in and, I surmised, since she had yet to allude once to the fact that she had caught me playing frantically with myself, it was probably the least I could do. When I agreed, her face cracked into a big smile and she got up to get ready. Try as I might, I couldn't take my eyes of her closely confined, chubby bum as she exited the kitchen.

Shopping with her was less of a drag than with my daughter, although she was wide-eyed at practically every dress she saw. She tried a few on and always wanted my opinion, and soon we were giggling away at her fashion-show impersonations. She had always been warm and blessed with humour, but our closeness that day, buoyed by our unmentioned secret, brought her to my attention as a sexual entity for the very first time. When she donned a LBD and did a mock catwalk parade, swinging her bum from side to side in an accentuated wiggle, I felt the familiar warmth radiating from my already tingling pussy.

The next shop proved to be the last in our hunt for clothes. We walked there arm in arm but silent, aware of the frisson between us. She tried on a tight-fitting dress in silver and black, and then called me down to the last cubicle in the fitting rooms to give my verdict. I pulled back the curtain and my jaw dropped open. She was perched on the narrow ledge, the skirt pulled up around her waist and her little knickers like a scrap of cloth at one ankle. Her legs were open and she was pumping two fingers deeply and methodically into the slit of her little pink pussy, letting me see all her seeping wetness, returning my favour from that morning.

Any efforts I could have mustered to think sensibly and avoid ravishing this delicious young thing – my own cousin's daughter – evaporated in an instant. I knew her eyes were open and on me, but I couldn't tear my gaze away from her tight, sticky puss.

'Please fuck me,' she breathed, 'I've never done it

before.'

I rushed her back into her clothes, and she fumbled at buttons in her bubbling excitement, seeing how flushed and eager I was to get her out of there so I could take her precious virginity. I pulled her to the counter and bought her the dress, and then took her by the hand and hurried her from the shop as she softly squealed with glee. Before we had even left the store I knew I was in trouble. My knickers were drenched and my pussy was insistent, but the realisation had dawned that my husband's golf would by now be over, and he would already be back at home.

This left a double problem: not only did we have nowhere to go, I also had no toys to use on her. Tongues and fingers had their place, but not for this, not for her first time; she needed a proper fucking. It made sense to delay our passions and arrange another time when we could be home alone, but by the look of her she would rather not wait, and I knew I certainly couldn't. I was already heading up the top end of the High Street as I racked my brain for a possible location. I didn't want to fuck her down some back alley or in the toilets of the shopping centre or a department store, but in reality, I knew I might have to resort to this. My pussy was hot and itching for action. I was absolutely gagging for her now, and letting this moment go was simply unthinkable.

If we continued, we could go to the park, site of one of the two lesbian experiences of my life to date. On my twentieth birthday and after much cider, my best friend had bent me over a fallen tree trunk, and finger-fucked me. Just as I began to come, grinding my crotch into the smoothly-weathered wood, she took her slick digits from me and slid one right up my arse. Back then it had been a warm spring evening, the park was all but deserted, and we were drunk. Today, with the heat of summer on us, the whole place would be a mass of sun seekers.

The top of the town was as empty as ever, and there was barely anyone around to witness me drag her into Imagine, the new adult store I'd yet to visit. It too was empty, staffed by a single goth girl, in her early twenties perhaps, her hair frizzed and dyed as black as her heavy eye make-up and coloured nails. She chewed her gum and watched us quizzically as I scoured the shelves for a likely implement within my budget to deflower the panting virgin by my side, if only I could think of somewhere to take her. Emma was speechless with excitement, handling the packets with awe as she tried to imagine the contents being used on her.

I was getting flustered, my mind flitting through countless dirty possibilities as each new toy and accessory was sighted. I wanted to paddle her spankable bum, clamp her teenage nipples, tease her clit by remote control, fill her with a double-ended dildo and shag myself silly too. Emma was right by my side, gripping me with anticipation as I tried to select the perfect dildo to fuck her with. The whole shop must have been filled with our desire for each other. It smelled like my bedroom after an afternoon of concerted masturbation. I don't think that ever, in my whole rude history, had I been more desperate for another person. I just hoped that I could drag myself past some of the quieter back streets to get her to the relative privacy of the department store toilets.

'Are you OK?' asked Goth Girl, which was a reasonable question since we looked far from OK; Emma was holding me and jiggling about, and I was fumbling through packets of toys like an addict at a drugstore counter.

'No!' I exclaimed without thinking. 'I need to fuck this girl before we both explode and I've got nowhere to take her!'

I knew I'd gone too far the moment I said it. Goth Girl turned on her heel and headed for the door, and my stomach churned as I realised we were going to be chucked out before I'd even had a chance to buy the toy we needed. I was so deflated I couldn't even plead, I just waited for her to open the door and demand our exit. But she didn't open it. She reached up and locked it instead. My heart was banging in my chest as she sauntered back towards us, a wicked smile forming on her lips, and said, 'Fuck her here. I want to watch you.'

Emma reacted quickest and was kissing me immediately, her tongue pushing into my mouth and swirling around. I was way too far gone to think of tender caresses. I grabbed and squeezed her tits and bottom, and then unbuttoned her cut-offs and pushed them down her thighs. As she stepped back to complete the removal of her shorts, Goth Girl behind me peeled my T-shirt up and over my head, then unclipped my bra to let my breasts bounce free and release my swollen nipples at last from their fabric constriction. My saviour then hurriedly stripped me of my skirt and knickers while I watched Emma, with only a tiny pause for modesty, also remove her damp underwear and cast it aside.

I didn't give her time to take off her top. I pulled her close and kissed her again, feeling our wet pussies bumping together. My hands were at her arse, finding the run of sweat in her crack and then the slimy touch of her free-flowing juices as my fingers searched downwards and dipped into the hot pool of her cunt from the rear. She gasped and grabbed my backside too, trying to replicate my probing movements and jabbing her finger against my tight anus in her hurry to find her way inside me. I didn't care, I just wanted filling. I pushed out to encourage deeper insertion but she had realised her mistake and burrowed her hand further between my cheeks to locate her true goal. She managed to get her tips inside me and rub my swollen labia as I ground against her.

Goth Girl wanted to direct proceedings, though. Wielding a dildo in a harness in one hand, she pulled Emma away by her hair and forced her on to all fours, giving me a first look at her plump, smooth-skinned bum opening up before me. I was handed the strap-on and saw that the fitted purple dildo was long and smooth, but nearly twice the girth of the one I had considered manageable for Emma's first time. But the juice was dripping from the young girl's puffy cunt, and the dildo had a shaped end to go up inside me, and I just couldn't stop myself from climbing into the harness and groaning with relief as the plastic slipped up into my sopping passage and nestled against the sweet spot within me.

I took Emma by the hips and slid slowly into her, hearing her cries but pushing relentlessly on, knowing how amazing it felt to be completely filled for the first time. As I paused to give her time to relax, Goth Girl let her lust overtake her too. She sucked and then bit my nipples, then grabbed a dispenser of tingling lube from the shelf and squeezed two dollops out onto my rock-hard teats. She deposited another thick dollop of lube onto her finger, spat with venom onto my tits, and then hungrily tongue-kissed me whilst reaching down into my deep crack and rubbing the minty lube on to my arse hole. She then broke off her kiss and spat into my open mouth. I didn't care – I wanted filth, the more of it the better.

112

Goth Girl left me and went off to grab a demonstration vibrator and a long black paddle from the counter. Then I held the wailing Emma firmly and took her virginity from her with deep, hard, bottom-slapping strokes that forced the yells from her throat and the cream from her pussy. As I fucked, Goth Girl smacked my arse hard with the paddle and called me a dirty lesbo whore, and made me ask for more punishment. The sting was sharp and shocking and set my bum on fire, but it was beautiful pain, and I didn't just ask for more, I begged for it.

I fucked hard, even though the plastic inside me and the press on the harness against my clit was making me come. The naughty shop-girl finally delivered Emma from her torment and applied the buzzing vibrator to her little clit, extracting wave after wave of climax until the young girl was entirely spent and forced herself off me to collapse on the floor. I still needed more, and Goth Girl was happy to oblige. She ran to another shelf and unboxed two more identical harnesses, both with a built-in moulded black cock. Still fully clothed, she fastened one to her waist and ordered the exhausted Emma to do the same.

I was ordered to climb on top of the shop girl, hold my pussy lips apart and then slide down the thickly-veined false prick. It was as big as any cock I have ever taken, but I was so wet and willing, my muscles just stretched and took it. I rode hard, holding my own tits and pinching the still tingling nipples as I jerked up and down. My second coming threatened to be bigger than my first and I had to stop and hold on, and to my frustration that arrested it, just before it hit its peak. As the tremors went through me, Goth Girl pulled me down close and pushed her tongue into my mouth once more.

I felt her hands squeezing my still-sore buttocks and

easing them apart. She pulled out of our snog and ordered Emma to get behind me. I realised with shock what was about to happen, but my pleas for mercy wouldn't leave my throat. Many years ago, before we were even married, my husband had once tried to put his cock up my bottom, but it had proved too much for me, and he abandoned his quest and had never tried again to this day. I screwed my eyes tight shut as I heard the next command from the cruel girl beneath me.

'Stick that cock right up her arse and fuck her with it,' she said.

I felt the blunt end of the dildo press against my minty-lubed anus. The pain was hard to bear. Emma pushed and I squeezed back against the invading plastic and tried to open up for it. My cries were loud but Emma knew no better and took them for ecstasy, pressing on with her mission until my muscles finally yielded. My nerve-endings came alive and I felt every single millimetre of the cock as it slid inexorably into me, and pain broke into unimaginable pleasure as both my hot holes were stuffed full.

I can't even remember how long they fucked me for, but I seemed to be coming every single second that my young cousin pumped into me and took the cherry I thought I would never lose. I was still half-delirious as Goth Girl unceremoniously made us dress and leave the shop so that she could tidy up and re-open. I do remember that outside the door, in broad daylight, Emma threw her arms around my neck, kissed me, and thanked me for taking her virginity. I smiled at her and then kissed her back, knowing this was just the start of something brilliant and secret between us.

'And thank you for taking mine,' I said.

City Girl, Country Girl
by Kristina Wright

"The Farmers Market is open!" Ellie screeched as she slammed the front door of our apartment. "Did you know this was opening weekend?"

Her words were accompanied by a little happy dance. Wiggling elbows and knees, she cha-cha chicken danced over to me on the couch and handed me the steaming coffee she'd gone to fetch for me from the corner coffee shop.

"Um, yeah, I guess," I mumbled. "I remember seeing a flyer about it. You didn't know?"

I yawned before taking a sip of my coffee. Two years of living with Ellie and I still wasn't used to her early-morning weekend cheerfulness. I chalked it up to growing up on a farm in Oklahoma. Ellie was a country girl through and through and I was a grumpily displaced New Yorker, still not quite used to the slower pace of Chicago, or as Ellie called it, "the big ol' city".

Ellie was bouncing from foot to foot like she had already downed a couple of triple-shot espressos. "No, I didn't know. Of course I didn't know! If I'd known, we would have been down there when they opened at six!"

"We?" I raised an eyebrow. "I love you, babe, but I would *not* be up at six for vegetables I can buy at the

115

store."

Ellie made a hurry-up rolling motion with her hand. "C'mon, c'mon. Stop complaining and let's go before all the best stuff is gone."

I wouldn't say her enthusiasm was exactly contagious, but it was after nine and I'd had my coffee, so I was feeling indulgent. She *was* kind of cute, my sweet bouncing Okie girl. "All right, I'm coming."

Ellie grabbed her "Go Green" tote bags – all four of them – and we headed down the street to the farmers market. Ellie was two steps ahead of me the entire way, falling back to let me catch up before her excitement propelled her forward once again. I may not have had much interest in the farmers market, but I did enjoy watching Ellie's bottom bounce and sway as she two-stepped up the busy street.

Yellow barricades blocked off the farmers market and streets normally filled with cars and cabs were converted into a pedestrian walkway. Stall after stall lined the street, with vendors hawking everything from fresh cut flowers to homegrown produce to local honey from beneath brightly coloured canopies. Ellie practically squealed in delight as she scooped up a bunch of fresh herbs and held it to her nose.

"Smell this, Anne," she said, holding a leafy green bundle out for me.

I took a whiff. It did smell good. "What is it?"

"Italian blend," the large woman behind the makeshift counter told us. "Oregano, basil, Italian parsley and marjoram. Great in a sauce or dried for later."

"I'll take two," Ellie said, fishing some money out of her pocket. "I know what I'm making for dinner."

My stomach rumbled. The only thing I "made" for dinner was reservations, but Ellie was a terrific cook. Her job in public relations for a nonprofit agency meant I hardly got to see her – and she hardly had time to cook. This farmers market idea was turning out to be a positive thing all away around.

Ellie had skipped ahead and was now buying a bevy of vegetables. I saw mushrooms, zucchini, squash and another bundle of herbs disappear into one of her tote bags. She held up a large red tomato for me to smell.

"These smell like real tomatoes, not those horrible store-bought ones."

I couldn't argue with her. The tomato *smelled* as ripe and juicy as it looked. It was only ten o'clock in the morning, but my mouth was already watering for whatever Ellie was making for dinner.

Another hour later and I was carrying a bouquet of sunflowers and a tote bag of fresh whole-wheat pasta and goat's milk cheese. The farmers market was winding down for the day and people wandered away with their purchases like ants at a banquet. I felt like I had spent a festive holiday in the country rather than a Saturday morning on a Chicago city street. Despite my initial reluctance, I found myself bouncing home with Ellie. Or as close to bouncing as I ever came.

Home again with our bounty, Ellie gave me a toe-curling kiss as she closed the door behind us. As always happens when my girl lays one on me, all rational thought flew out of my mind as I focused on her soft mouth against mine. Somewhere in there, the bags we were carrying fell to the ground with a thump-thud-thump as I pressed Ellie against the door. She moaned into my mouth, that breathy little sound that let me know I was getting to her. Getting her wet, getting her as juicy as those ripe tomatoes she'd bought that were now rolling across the floor.

I pulled back, but only slightly, and murmured against her lips, "What was that for?"

She licked my bottom lip. "For going to the market with me."

I cupped her luscious bottom in my hands and gave it a squeeze. "I see. Well, I did leave the house awfully early on a Saturday morning. All I get is a kiss?"

Nibbling my collarbone, she giggled. "Well, it was a *good* kiss."

"No argument here," I said. "But, you know, I could have been reading the paper or napping ..."

She looked up at me, lips twitching with barely suppressed laughter. "I see. So, you think your reward should be something more ... substantial?"

I smacked her ass, hard enough to make her squeak. "Maybe."

Ellie may be shorter and thinner than me, but she's quick. She somehow managed to sweep my legs out from under me so that I was on my back on the hardwood floor. She landed on top of me, all angles and planes. I let out something a little louder than a squeak when one of her bony elbows made contact with my ribs. She giggled, shifting on me in a way that was a little less dangerous and a little more delicious.

I looked up into her sea-green eyes; her blonde braids flopping down either side of my face. "You're a bad girl."

She winked at me. "You don't know the half of it."

Stretching for one of the oversized tomatoes she'd acquired on our shopping trip, she hefted it in her hand before taking a bite. Tomato juice oozed between her fingers, down her wrist and across my T-shirt.

"Hey, Okie, you're getting me all wet."

She held the tomato out for me to take a bite. "That's

kinda the point," she said, all breathy, as if sharing a tomato was the sexiest thing she'd ever done. "Take a bite."

I'm not a big fan of raw vegetables, but I did as she said. The tomato squished across my tongue, the sweet-acidic taste trickling down my throat. It tasted better than any store-bought tomato I'd ever had. I licked my lips and smiled.

"Not bad."

Ellie sat up and fished through one of the tote bags. "Wait until you try this honey. It's incredible."

She extracted the wooden dipper and trickled the honey across my closed lips. I opened my mouth to protest and got a taste of what I imagined liquid sunshine might taste like. She giggled at my expression.

"Told you."

I pulled her down on top of me, kissing her with my honeyed lips. "Yeah, you did. What else you got in that bag?"

She had a tough time responding because my hands were under her T-shirt, pulling it over her head with one hand while I pinched her nipples lightly with the other. "Good stuff," she gasped. "All kinds of good stuff."

I squirmed under her and took a plump nipple in my mouth. I moaned against her sun-warmed skin, sucking until she whimpered low in her throat. Then I rolled her over on the floor, one of the "Go Green" totes crinkling underneath her. I made quick work of her shorts and panties and sat back to admire my work. Spread out amidst the produce and flowers, she looked like the dessert at the end of a decadent meal.

I extracted a dark green zucchini from her bag of goodies. With a wicked grin, I ran it down between her breasts and across her stomach. She gasped as I stroked her between the thighs with the sizeable veggie.

"You wouldn't," she taunted.

"Wouldn't I?"

I didn't give her time to respond. I nudged the rounded end of the zucchini between the glistening lips of her pussy, watching the way it opened her. She arched her back and the end of the vegetable slipped inside her wetness. I pumped it slowly, fingering her clit in lazy circles, enjoying the naughty image of an innocent farm girl being debauched by produce.

Eyes closed, back arched, Ellie wasn't ready for what I did next. Grabbing up a bundle of her Italian herbs, I quickly withdrew the zucchini and slapped the green bunch across her bare pussy. It wasn't a hard slap, but the sensation was enough to make her yelp and then laugh.

"That stings and tickles," she said.

I took that as a good sign and did it again. Liking the way she yelped and squirmed, but didn't close her legs, I did it again. The bruised herbs released their fragrance and blended with the delicious scent of her pussy. I chuckled. "It smells like an Italian whorehouse in here."

In a throaty voice I barely recognised, Ellie said, "Well, fuck me then. I want you to get your money's worth."

I shucked my clothes and covered Ellie's naked body with my own. "Hey, little country girl, what's that?" I asked, as I reached between us to thumb her swollen clit. "You're awfully excited."

"Farmers markets get me hot. Didn't you know that?" She bucked against me. "Fuck me."

I shimmied down her body and took up the zucchini once more. She spread her legs eagerly, staring into my eyes as the zucchini entered her and spread her open. I pumped it inside her, getting turned on by the wet sounds her pussy made as I withdrew it. Her juices glistened halfway up the length of the long vegetable, leaving streaks of opalescence along the dark green skin. It was naughty and erotic as hell to watch my Okie girl writhe against the zucchini.

"Yes, oh yes," she gasped, gripping my hair as I fucked her.

She threw back her head, her body straining toward orgasm. Her hands tightened in my hair, pulling me toward her crotch. I took it as an invitation and leaned over her, sucking her clit between my lips. I gave her short, quick thrusts with the zucchini as I sucked her rigid clit, tonguing it in between. That was enough to send her over the edge. Clinging to my hair and wrapping her lean thighs around my head, she came, smelling of herbs and vegetables, fresh air and arousal.

I slowly withdrew the zucchini from her clinging pussy as I kept lapping at her clit. She whimpered and moaned, torn between pulling me closer because it felt so good and pushing me away because the sensation was too intense. It was a familiar battle I'd seen play out before and I enjoyed every moment of it, drawing as much pleasure from licking her as she was receiving. Finally, with a deep moan, she pushed me away. Doubled up and gasping as if she'd just run a marathon, she stroked my head like I was an obedient puppy who had just brought her the newspaper.

"Oh, oh, my," she murmured, trying to catch her breath. "That was delicious."

I licked my lips, tasting her and still caught in the web of my own arousal. "Yes, it was."

She looked around us at the mess we'd made; the vegetables scattered across the room, the honey dripping onto the wood floor, the crushed herbs and mushrooms.

121

Then she laughed. "So much for dinner."

I reached for her, pulling her into my arms and directing her hand between my thighs. "I'm only hungry for one thing right now."

As she slid two fingers inside me, she sighed. "Well, the farmers market is open tomorrow, too, if you want to go."

At that moment, straining against her sweat-slick body as she touched just the way I liked, I couldn't think of anything else I'd rather do on a Sunday morning.

Symmetry
by Jeremy Edwards

At times, Carla thought it was the mind-blowing symmetry that made her crave Susan's body night after night, fifteen years into their partnership.

It was love that accounted for the fact that they were spending a lifetime together. Carla knew this. But when the atmosphere in their bedroom shifted from overhead fixture to little pink bedside lamp, was it love, per se, that made her intent on getting her tongue inside Susan's mouth and her fingers inside Susan's pussy, before either of them considered sleep?

Or was it the never-ending attraction of fucking her mirror image ...

Early on, when they used to hit the clubs together every weekend, people had constantly mistaken them for sisters. It was more than just their similar body types (boyish), hair colour (natural blonde), and noses (button). It was the way they each moved and gestured. And a way they exchanged knowing looks and sympathetic smiles. And jokes that others found to be impenetrable.

Perhaps there had also been an element of wishful thinking on the part of all those club boys and girls who wanted to fuck them. Maybe they didn't want to see that those looks and smiles and jokes signified a connection even more intimate than the kind shared by siblings.

Hell, even their current landlady had asked if they were sisters, and that was within the past year. Over housewarming wine, Susan and Carla had speculated pleasantly about what, and in precisely what manner, the handsome homeowner had hoped to do her new tenants.

They had matured right in step with each other, not only emotionally but also physically. The same still-nearly-invisible grey hairs, appearing unannounced. The same subtle thickening of the body, from "slight" to "svelte". The same little lines around each woman's mouth, which identified the wearer as someone who laughed long, hard, and often.

Carla would never forget the first time Susan stripped for her, poised daintily in her bedroom with a smile that said "I'm shy" but a glimmer and resolve in her eye that said "I'm going to eat and drink you up, honey, then eat and drink you up again for dessert." That look had made Carla so wet, and she had stood there for a sacred moment, her pulse frozen and her panties clinging. And in that moment, she had found that one thought in particular stood out from all the giddiness, marvel, and lust: *she looks like me.* Before, this had been something to take for granted. But here it had emerged as the most arousing revelation she'd ever had.

Is that what my pussy looks like when it's wet? Carla would often think as she held Susan's tender lips apart, before tasting her. After fifteen years, the thought still did it for her. Sometimes she would stop to rub Susan's blonde bush, then her own blonde bush, alternating the soft strokes with perfect equity. *One for me ... one for you ...* until Susan, gliding on giggles, would clutch gently at Carla's furry mound and elicit a parallel river of laughter. Carla would sneak a look at the mirror on the wall and see two 41-year-old beauties with their hands between each other's legs. She would observe Susan's bottom wiggling with titillated abandon and her own face flushing with pleasure. Sometimes, when they were sufficiently entangled, she couldn't tell whose legs were whose. At those moments, they had a collective resemblance to some many-limbed goddess, transported by secret joys.

Susan worked in an office, and Carla worked at home. Every evening Susan would arrive, give her lover a quick kiss and a lingering ass-squeeze, and head down the hall to change. Susan would always begin to shed her jeans or skirt before reaching the bedroom. Sometimes, if the day had been humid, the panties would also begin a downward journey before she veered out of sight. *Is that what my pretty ass looks like when I'm striding down the hall?* Carla would wonder. She would touch herself while waiting for Susan to return.

And yet, the symmetry was in many ways illusory. Fifteen years in, Carla knew that she and Susan did not make decisions the same way, experience emotions the same way, or process information the same way. And though their tone and timbre of voice showed a sisterly affinity, they rarely expressed themselves in the same words.

Oh, they were compatible, all right – securely and deliciously so. But large chunks of the compatibility grew out of their differences rather than their similarities. Strong suits to vulnerabilities, expertise here to ingenuousness there … how well they complemented each other.

How well, indeed. In the bedroom, Carla, who couldn't care less about having her nipples licked, could make Susan come by licking hers. The alien nature of

Susan's pleasure, in Carla's eyes, made it especially exciting to deliver, even to anticipate. *I am in love with a woman who is creaming to have her nipples licked tonight.*

In the very midst of gratifying that desire, Carla would reflect on it, and she would feel her arousal grow with the tangible awareness of Susan's distinctness from her. The ecstasy of bringing Susan to ecstasy was itself sometimes more pleasure than Carla knew what to do with, and she would simply come in her panties, slickly and helplessly, before Susan could even touch her.

But Susan would touch her, and Carla had taught her where to do so. The place was just barely south of her clit – not part of the clit, but an infinitesimal distance away – a signature locus along her inner lips, a unique receptor for an impossibly cozy type of bliss, like mulled wine and warm bathwater and slow-motion orgasms, that was not quite comparable to any of the rich sensations that emanated from her tingling bud or her pulsing cunt walls. Carla may have been the only woman in the world with a special nerve ending exactly there; she cherished it, and Susan could sensually pamper her merely by breathing on it awhile. In fact, she was expected to, night after night.

Vive la différence! Carla liked to say, with a passionate irony, to her same-sex near-twin, when Susan put her over the edge. The French words came out in a guttural slur as Carla's cunt trembled around fingers that looked very much like her own, but moved so differently.

Tonight was the night the landlady had invited them for dinner. But they'd taken a rain check, because this was their anniversary. That morning, Susan had dressed both for the office and for home – the skirt suit was one of her

126

most elegant workaday outfits, but it was understood, when the suit came off, that the sight of Susan in ruffled blouse and burgundy panty-hose would especially please Carla. Carla was the type to buy a present; Susan was the type to dress up.

This evening, Carla could see that Susan was walking more slowly than usual as she sauntered down the hall, intentionally taking her time as she slithered out of her skirt. Carla grabbed the gift from the coffee table and ran down the hall after her, catching her with a waist-gripping gesture of possession, accompanied by the pressure of her mound against Susan's panty-hose-perfect ass. She knew that Susan, who was always very deliberate, was turned on by her impulsiveness.

Susan spun around, kicked her skirt out of the way, and smiled at Carla. Then she accepted the small, rectangular package that her woman was extending to her.

"You know," she kidded, "there's a part of me that never wants to open presents. Until it's unwrapped, a present represents perfect fulfilment of every wish, doesn't it?"

Carla's eyes roamed over Susan, relishing the seductive effect of the translucent tights, through which the outrageous understatement of a silken, minimalist thong was revealed. She glanced at the skirt that relaxed, two feet away, on the floor. "My present's unwrapped," she said. "And it represents perfect fulfilment of every wish."

Susan found Carla's mouth with her own – they fitted each other precisely, a matched set – and they shared their breath for a minute.

Then Carla gently took the unopened present out of Susan's hand. "This isn't perishable," she explained. "It's

127

not fragile, either." And she tossed it onto the floor, letting Susan's skirt cushion the impact.

Tonight, they did it right in the hallway.

Having relieved Susan of the package, Carla pulled her to the floor. She was torn between the almost fetishistic appeal of caressing, wrestling, even humping Susan in her burgundy panty-hose … and the overwhelming desire to crinkle the panty-hose down her legs, pull aside the thong, and get her face in touch with the fragrant, liquid core of Susan's womanhood.

Reason told her to enjoy Susan in the hose while she could – because, once peeled down, they would certainly not be going back on. Not tonight.

The thrill of petting Susan into a state of hyper-arousal, while she was still contained within the burgundy shell, rewarded Carla's nod to reason. Her lover's legs, which she knew like her own, seemed to churn and ripple beneath her touch. And when she stroked across the crotch of the panty-hose, she felt fire.

Carla knew how it felt to go moist in a tiny thong – that precious feeling of one's sexuality overwhelming one's apparel – and as she inched the panty-hose down to reveal Susan's squirming, tender flesh, the sight connected like a doorbell to her own thong. Once again, Carla indulged the convenient sensory luxury of loving a partner who was her physical double.

Just as she'd imagined doing, she pulled the thong aside, rather than removing it. She held Susan within the silk frame like a flower in a hatband, licking and stroking the open petals, which displayed themselves for her as if some gifted milliner had arranged everything to perfection.

Susan's ecstasy made a sticky mess on Carla's face, like a fruit cocktail consumed in haste. As Carla lapped up every nurturing drop, Susan cried, softly and joyously. Carla, who often laughed when she came, felt her heart throbbing for this girl who cried when she came.

Susan always drifted off before Carla. Tonight, as every night, Carla held her lover tightly, her arms surrounding Susan's bottom. She framed the placid globes, presenting them to herself to love with a hundred soft kisses. She gradually lulled herself by grazing on the fleshy, passive cheerfulness of the beloved ass. *Your ass in my arms, your cheeks in my face.* The thought, and the reality, guaranteed sweet dreams.

Yes, tonight had been an anniversary, a special night, a night for politely declining a landlady's invitation. But the landlady might have been surprised to know just how regularly these two women long in love, sharing the same years, the same looks, and the same lifetime, were fucking each other's matching behinds off through layers of symmetry and deeper layers of individuality … stripping away at their sameness and uncovering the raw elements of erotic essence.

The landlady might have been surprised.

Holiday Camp Sharing
by Mark Farley

"Center Parcs? We really are a pair of old dykes, aren't we?"

"What's that supposed to mean, Alys?" Dahlia shot back at me scornfully as we arrived in Sherwood Forest. That's my girlfriend. My partner, actually. God, I keep forgetting. As of two weeks ago, she is (technically) my wife. *My wife.* That's right. My beautiful black princess with her long slender legs and her little bubble bottom. Her cascading, weaved curls of many colours. Me with my bad dress sense, not to mention my stumpy and very pale frame. *Oh Gosh.* I still think that's so amazing that we are able to – you know, like the whole civil partnership thing.

I still can't believe she asked me, and the day after the law passed too. I mean, we'd only been dating six months but I guess when you know, you know. *Right?*

She took me completely unawares. It was an *OK* day, not really picnic weather but a bunch of us went out onto the Heath anyway and as we stopped throwing the Frisbee around like children and settled down to some Cava and mini sausage rolls, she chose to pop the question. I cried. So did my friends.

Our wedding day was so perfect. The sun shone down on the Town Hall square in Brighton and there was such a great vibe from the locals too, who had probably seen this every day. They milled around politely with their takeaway coffees and watched with respect and joy as we stood there, smiling for the camera in our specially tailored threads. So many of our loved ones showed up for our reception in the spacious atrium of the nearby Thistle. What a day to remember!

"What do I mean?" I answered Dahlia, cocksure and intending to amuse her. "I mean, coming somewhere like this for our honeymoon. We are such a pair of old hens … What on earth are we going to here?"

"I thought it only mattered who we were with. I think that's more important …"

"Of course, Hun …" I cooed. We walked through the Village Square side by side, en route to the Reception, negotiating our suitcases around the oblivious families and numerous buggies and pushchairs that darted into our paths.

"Anyway," she snapped, digging me in the ribs. "Watch who you are calling old …"

Dahlia hates it when I refer to her age in any context because she's, like, twelve years older than me and is always acutely aware of the gap. Like when we met, I had to pursue her for weeks to get a second date because she was so wary of dating someone much younger. I don't care though. I love her the way she is and, besides, it's not like she's even forty yet.

We went up to Reception to check into our Woodland Lodge still giggling together, and we proceeded to take the piss out of one another, and the new surroundings that we had chosen to be our home, for the whole of the next week.

"Not everything we do has to revolve around our normal haunts and circle of friends, y'know. We can manage at least one trip that doesn't revolve around a Pride march," she reasoned with me.

I assumed she was referring to the summer before when I spoke of my desire to visit America for the first time, and our stay in the three different cities we visited that June coincided with Gay Pride events that were already planned.

She did have a point, though. If it's not the local LGBT BBQ, quiz or chess night, it's some sort of girls-only club arrangement that we frequent of a wine-soaked evening. But then everywhere seems to have a Pride event these days. There are even two in Texas!

"Why not go somewhere different?" she had joked, when we sat down and planned our nuptials all that time ago. "Mix with the rest of the world …"

"Hey …" I nodded nonchalantly at the people behind us. "We might not be alone in this camp, after all."

Dahlia turned (perhaps a little too obviously) and a look of uncomfortable paranoia came over the two women who had just entered the cramped office They were similar-looking brunettes in their thirties. I sensed the awkward moment we had created and tried my best to beam one of my winning smiles at them.

A look of relief replaced the mild horror and as we all carried on waiting I noticed that they were chatting in German. I raised an eyebrow at my partner and she reciprocated with the sort of knowing glance that said I should not doubt her organisational skills but also hoped that we would make their acquaintance.

Now, as appealing as the idea of just escaping with Dahlia, away from the capital and the usual scene, was, a little action with some like-minded souls didn't lack appeal either. What with the military organisation of events that was necessary for our special day, we hadn't had a curious fumble with anyone else for a while, not even with any of our regular circle of occasional late-night visitors.

Because we're not that sort of couple: really intense and insistent on monogamy. We just go ahead and appreciate what life offers from time to time and, with that in mind, I waited for the opportune time to introduce myself to our fellow holidaymakers. I decided to wait until Dahlia began the procedure at the desk before I feigned boredom and cracked a bad joke about my partner being the one who wears the trousers. They laughed.

"She is too," one nodded to the other, jokingly.

"Magda," she hissed, pretending to be appalled.

"Oh, you have names too ..." I giggled. Dahlia looked back from the desk and smiled, rolling her eyes at them in response to my fooling.

Magda and (as I soon found out) Christine live in a small town just outside Munich. I asked them if they had ever been to London. They hadn't but wanted to come soon. We told them how much we loved places like The Candy Bar. Both girls looked at each other and smiled, clearly acknowledging they were aware of the notorious, Soho pick-up joint.

As Magda replaced Dahlia in front of the increasingly sour-faced check-in girl, Christine hung back with us and continued to tell us about the scene in Munich, in cheeky subtle whispers so as not to broadcast our lifestyle to the rest of the room. This was cute and also exciting. It was clear to us all that we had run into kindred spirits. Their clubs sounded a lot tamer than ours, but she assured us

133

that this bred a healthy online community of swingers and privately arranged meetings. I asked her why they had come to such a place and not ventured to somewhere like London instead.

"We've been coming here for years," admitted Christine. "We just love the woodland. Magda's family brought her here as a child."

Magda came back just as she spoke and rolled her eyes in geek-laden shame at her girlfriend's admission. Dahlia immediately put a sympathetic arm around Magda and chuckled away, in order to cover her embarrassment a little.

We chatted for a time before arranging to meet later for dinner.

"There's a really great Indian on the camp, if you are going out later …. We'll be there," Christine offered.

The two of us looked at each other and raised our eyebrows in curiosity.

"Sure.. 7pm?"

"I can't believe we have picked up here!" Dahlia laughed later on as we changed for the restaurant. We agreed to keep things simple. I opted for shorts and T-shirt, but Dahlia pulled out her favourite handkerchief top she reserves for when we are out on the pull. The one that shows off her entire, gorgeous back and tribal tattoo and the base of her spine. She finished it off with a denim mini and flip-flops. Her intentions for the rest of the evening seemed clear!

The girls had already ordered wine for the table and were looking through menus by the time we walked in, hand in hand and fifteen minutes late. Magda and Christine seemed to clock our proud, public display of affection and looked a little uncomfortable. Dahlia embraced Magda and gave her a friendly kiss on the lips. The German reeled a little at this and looked a bit stunned as she sat back in her seat. I waved at the couple, awkwardly and giggled. We exchanged pleasantries and they seemed to warm up slightly.

"We took the liberty of ordering the "Shuruati …whats-it," Christine said as she poured glasses of wine out for us. "It's a shared platter of starters … We weren't sure what you'd like …"

"We're into most things!" announced my partner, cheekily.

The passanda's and dopazia's soon arrived and we tucked in. I felt aroused at the smells as well as the sight of fingers being licked and used in place of cutlery. It wasn't long before we charmed them and soon enough we were chatting like old mates.

It was getting dark by the time we left the restaurant. All four of us looked up at the brilliant night sky. We were unused to being able to see the stars so bright; without the diluting light of the city. We were all heading back in the same general direction and our two new friends led the way, casually glancing back to see that we were heading the same way. I took Dahlia's hand and moved in to rest my head on her shoulder. She kissed the top of my head and let go of my hand to fondle my arse through my skirt, as there was nobody else around. I caught the odd word from the two girls in front of us, hoping that they were discussing what they wanted to do with us. I was sure I heard a 'fuck' and a 'from behind' in amongst their stifled giggles. They stopped, hand in hand at a junction.

'I think we part here …" announced Magda, glancing

at her partner. "Unless, of course, you would like to walk us home …"

"Sure, we can do that," announced Dahlia confidently, without waiting for me. As we made our way up their path, I released Dahlia's hand and made up the short distance between us. I slotted myself in between them and put an arm around each of their waists.

"So, which one of you beautiful ladies am I going to get to kiss first?" I teased.

"How about both of us?" answered Christine. She turned towards me and took my arm, placing it onto her bottom. She took my face in both her hands and gave me a long, deep kiss. Magda stood close to one side and Christine broke off to place a kiss on the mouth of her partner, who too broke away and guided her girlfriend's lips on to mine in a lovely three-way cocktail. Dahlia hung back and admired the sight in front of her, purring.

"What a lovely view …"

Christine moved towards her and embraced my lover.

It was a good job we were just around the corner from their chalet because we were all getting quite excited and eager to progress further, as we walked up hand in hand with our newfound partners. Dahlia gave me a slow, wide-eyed look and chuckled to herself.

Christine played host, popping a cork on something white and sparkling. We stood around the double bed, awkwardly chatting for a while before Magda broke the ice and pulled her dress over her head and sighing, "That's better …" and leaving herself very much nude. She picked up her glass again from the top of the TV, which I noticed hadn't even been turned on during their stay, as the remote was still in its makeshift plastic holder, by the pay-per-view menu.

Magda had an ample body she was clearly very

comfortable with. Her partner took a seat on the bed and reached out for her. She cupped one of her breasts and muttered, "Isn't she beautiful?"

"That she is," replied Dahlia from behind her and moved in, wrapping her arms around her and nuzzling at her neckline. I also leaned forward for a kiss as Christine scooted backwards on the bed to watch the action unfold. I stepped out of my shorts and joined her for a snog, reaching my hand down the front of her jeans. Dahlia led Magda by the hand and shooed the two of us over to the other half of the bed, so we could all fit on.

Almost immediately, I felt the cheeky hand of Magda wandering over from embracing my lover to touch the crack of my arse. She searched around and slipped a finger into my hole as she tongued Dahlia's sweet mouth. By the moans coming from her, I sensed that my baby had a few fingers of her own buried in somewhere wet and warm behind me. Christine, on the other hand, was sucking one of my boobs and joining Magda in fingering my cunt.

I sensed someone getting up and opened my eyes to see Dahlia excusing herself to go to the bathroom. She gave me a wink from the foot of the bed, so I carried on. Magda turned to join us and spooned me from behind, while her partner and I rubbed one another's crotch.

As Dahlia returned, she undid the neck-straps of her top and watched Magda lean over me and kiss her partner. I reached out a hand to Dahlia, now naked and sipping her drink. She kicked off her heels and climbed on to the bed to join us.

She gave me a wonderful, deep kiss that displayed a relaxed confidence, which I was glad about. I was so proud of how instantly she had been at ease with all this, not seeming threatened or bothered at all. It relaxed me enough so that I could really enjoy myself too. Something I was more than planning on doing.

Christine rose from her position to replenish her drink. Magda howled with laughter.

"You OK?" I asked her.

"Yeah, she makes fun of me because I am always the last person to undress …"

Magda broke off from kissing Dahlia and announced, "Get naked then!"

We all joined in and I seconded her demand for nudity.

"Would you like some help?" I joked as she unbuttoned her shirt and peeled the tight jeans over her bum.

"Yes, you can get on the edge of the bed and open your legs …" she ordered. Dahlia looked up and watched me dutifully shift down to the edge of the bed, where Christine was crouched in her mismatched cotton bra and pants. She and Magda were watching intently and sipping from their glasses.

"She gives head like you would not imagine," muttered Magda.

"Oooo, there's a challenge …" I motioned down to Christine, with her juicy fingers up my pussy lips. "I've had a lot of great head in my time …"

She wasn't far wrong. I got a delicious combination of clit-sucking and finger-darting that warmed me up considerably. She then concentrated on massaging my inside wall, just on the spot I love. It wasn't long before she had me making the right noises and making my hips buck wildly. I grabbed the back of her head and pulled her into me, encouraging her to continue.

I looked up and demanded that one of the others sit on my face. My gorgeous, dark beauty obliged without batting an eyelid. She rode away on my tongue as Magda fingered her bottom from behind, occasionally bending down to where Christine was lapping away.

At this opportunity, I took Dahlia and got into a lovely 69. I ejaculated onto her face as I straddled over her and screamed into her groin; she purred lovingly somewhere beneath me. The other girls retreated to a couch across the room and brought each other off, kneeling in front of one another with grins on their faces as they enjoyed our display.

They looked deep into each other's eyes and they made each other cum with a close intimacy I envied but could also recognise in our own relationship. They grasped each other, creating a light film of sweat that blended into a lovely cocktail as they embraced and rubbed at each other furiously until climax. They writhed and gasped and rode each other's caress until they collapsed into one another's arms. They laughed a little uncomfortably as they realised we'd been watching and sheepishly hopped on to the bed to hide their heads in our embraces. We lay in a wonderful after-shag trance, drank the bottle dry and then enjoyed the rest of our night with them.

Center Parcs, I'd recommend it to anyone!

Japanese Schoolgirls
by Teresa Joseph

For as long as I can remember, I've always known that in my heart that I'm a lesbian. And since the age of about fourteen or fifteen when my classmates started wearing push-up bras and the shortest skirts that they could get away with, I've known that I have perverted lust for adult women in school uniform. But five months ago, while I was downloading a few 'sexy schoolgirl' videos from the Internet, I came across something that made me wank so hard that I've never been able to stop.

At first glance of course, there wasn't anything particularly horny about this video; just a ten-second clip of an adult Japanese schoolgirl grinning from ear to ear as she wrote "I love you" on a blackboard before bending over to give us a flash of her knickers. But although she didn't really do anything, the schoolgirl was so gorgeous that, after a few moments, the computer screen was completely covered in lipstick and I was addicted for life.

Within thirty minutes of downloading the clip, I'd signed up to every "Adult Japanese Schoolgirl" website on the internet and fingered my pussy until I saw stars, watching a bevy of pretty young Orientals in skimpy school uniforms giggle with delight as they eagerly touched each other's naked pussies. But no matter how much I wanked or how many videos I downloaded, I knew that there was only one thing that was going to satisfy my aching pussy and my drooling tongue. And so a few days later, having almost literally *begged* my boss to let me take some holiday time, I jumped on to the very next flight to Tokyo and drove myself mad with anticipation as I spent the next thirteen hours waiting to touch down.

Were the Fates playing some cruel practical joke at my expense? Why else would they decide to seat me in a section of the plane surrounded by more than a half a dozen *real* Japanese schoolgirls in full school uniform who were on their way home to Japan?

Japan is the only country in the world where the students don't graduate from secondary education until after they've turned 21. And judging by the gold badges on their lapels, not to mention their gorgeous figures, it was obvious that every one of these girls was in their last year of school.

They were all so irresistibly sexy that the urge to kiss and fuck every one of them senseless was almost completely overwhelming. And as I sat there, mere inches away from their gorgeous bodies, almost cumming every time that I heard them giggle and wishing that I could touch their skin, I had no choice but to sit there as rigid as a statue and *pray* that I didn't end up getting arrested for sexual assault.

The honey was dripping from my pussy like water out of a tap. My legs were crossed so tightly that I was starting to get a cramp. I was so afraid of groaning or whimpering with lust that I bit my tongue for hours on end. And knowing that it was only a matter of time before I'd try to do something that would get me arrested, I kept my eyes shut as tightly as I could and kept my hands crossed in my lap, looking so tense that the stewardess offered me a sedative because she thought I was afraid of flying.

I refused of course, doing my best to dismiss the whole thing and saying that I would be fine. But when the schoolgirl sitting next to me turned to ask me if I was all right, I honestly began to wish that I'd taken the sedative after all.

"Are, you, O-*K*?" She asked in broken English, but in a tone so sweet and melodious that it actually made me cum. And as I sat there whimpering like a frightened puppy, I couldn't help but groan with orgasm as she reached out to touch my hand and caress my long blonde hair.

According to the dictionary, ambivalence is a mental state in which a person experiences two separate emotions at the same moment in time. But actually sitting there in economy class, so stricken with terror that I almost started to hyperventilate but so driven by lust that it was hard for me not to kiss her gorgeous lips, I was positive that there had to be a Hell of a lot more to it than that.

After six hours of this torture I was absolutely certain that if I didn't have a wank soon then I was going to explode. And since a nervous aeroplane passenger dashing off to the toilets was the most natural thing in the world, a few minutes later I was sitting on the toilet seat with my knees pulled up around my ears, fisting my pussy so furiously that I had to bite my other hand.

For ten, long, exhaustive minutes, I pounded my pussy until the hot, sweet honey was literally gushing like water from a fountain. But then, just as I thought that I might be able to satisfy myself, I heard a knock on the door that made me groan "Oh God No" as I started wanking even harder than before.

"Lady? Are you, O-K?" Asked the gorgeous schoolgirl, obviously worried by all the groaning and gasping and believing that something was wrong.

I tried to answer, to say that I was fine and that I'd be out in a minute, but I was wanking too hard to even catch my breath. And a few moments later, something terrible happened that somehow actually managed to make me even hornier than before.

Whether I'd forgotten to lock the door or if there was some kind of 'override button' that the stewardesses could use in an emergency, before I knew it, the Japanese schoolgirl was actually watching me wank. And as my pussy ejaculated for the seventh time in a row, the look of pure shock and disbelief on her face soon turned to one of childish curiosity as she began to giggle at what she saw.

At the beginning of my favourite 'Adult Japanese Schoolgirl' videos, a gang of giggling classmates always watch from the doorway as the two girls quietly fuck each other, unaware of the fact that they are being watched. And now, as a gorgeous, giggling schoolgirl stood watching me in real life, the thrill I received was so intense that the next time I ejaculated, some of the honey actually splashed onto the front of her skirt.

It was only at that moment that I actually realised what I'd done, how I had deliberately left the door unlocked in the hopes that this might happen. And so when it looked as if the girl was actually rushing back to her seat, I was so terrified by the thought that she might not come back that, despite my exhaustion, I actually reached out to her with my hand and begged her not to go.

Luckily however, as it turned out the schoolgirl was

just dashing back to her friends to say something along the lines of, "Hey, come and see what the white lady is doing. It's really funny." Because the next thing I knew, I was on the verge of passing out as more than half a dozen giggling schoolgirls all crowded around the toilet's doorway, curious to see a woman fist herself unconscious.

I couldn't understand a word of what they were saying, but the sound of their voices still thrilled me so much that I couldn't have stopped wanking if I'd tried. But from the way that they were giggling and coaxing each other, it was clear that they were saying something along the lines of, "Go on. I dare you. I *double* dare you." And with my fist still buried wrist-deep inside my pussy, I whimpered with anticipation and my heart skipped a beat as I wondered what it was that they were daring each other to do.

In the end of course, the girl who stepped forward was so beautiful that I wanted to spend the rest of my life with her, or at the very least, to kiss her gorgeous ruby lips until I passed out with delight. So when she slowly bent forward to kiss me on the lips, it was more satisfying than anything that you can imagine. And as she reached out her delicate porcelain fingers to touch my smooth, naked pussy, I yelped with overwhelming ecstasy, there was a flash of white light, and then everything went dark.

When at last I finally woke up, a stewardess was knocking on the door to tell me that the seatbelt sign was on and that I had to return to my seat. And although I was in a panic about returning to the seat in such a terrible state, it turned out that the schoolgirls were even more conscientious then I'd thought.

*   *   *

While I was unconscious, the girls had actually brushed my hair for me and reapplied my makeup. And since my own skirt and knickers had been completely soaked with honey, the girls had left them in a plastic bag and dressed me in one of the short blue pleated skirts and a pair of the white cotton knickers that I had lusted after for so long.

So needless to say, with legs as long as mine, I received quite a few lustful leers from the men on the plane as I skipped back to my seat, bent over to push the plastic bag into the bin.

As I sat down to fasten my seatbelt, smiling gratefully at all of the Japanese schoolgirls who were seated around me, I struggled in vain to remember the Japanese word for "Thank you." And once we had touched down at the airport and I was forced to wave goodbye to all of my new friends, I would have given almost anything to spend my life with them.

As it was however, I was now standing in the heart of a city where gorgeous 18+ Japanese schoolgirls were an everyday fact of life, wearing a skirt so short that my knickers were visible while I was standing up. And although I didn't even have a change of clothes, I was too busy fantasising about Japanese pussy to really give a damn.

I'd been in such a rush to get to Japan that I hadn't even bothered to pack a suitcase. But luckily however, I still had my credit card and a few hundred pounds in cash that I could convert to Japanese yen. And so having bought myself a new knee-length skirt and pair of black satin knickers from a handy airport store, I went out to the nearest taxi stand and set out to fulfil my dream.

From one of the 10,000 Adult Schoolgirl websites that I had joined a couple of nights before, I'd printed off an address in Japanese that I sincerely hoped would make my dreams come true.

Of course, it could have just been the address of a five-star sushi restaurant, but from the look on the female taxi driver's face when she read the address, it was clear that I was on the right track. And so having driven out to a short, narrow alley that it would have taken me a hundred years to find on my own, the taxi driver took 15,000 yen from my purse and then drove off into the night, leaving me staring at the flashing neon signs of this hidden business and praying that I was in the right place.

The thought that the taxi driver might indeed have dumped me outside a sushi restaurant and left me to fend for myself made me feel so nervous that I was too afraid to even step through the front door. But, as the sexiest Japanese schoolgirl that I've ever seen in my life, having obviously dealt with a lot of shy first-timers in the past, came out to greet me and to invite me inside, I came with delight, completely ruining my new black knickers.

"Hi! You American?" She asked so cheerfully that I fell in love on the spot.

"Err, no … English." I gasped excitedly, too mesmerized by her gorgeous body to even string together a coherent sentence.

"You look for grown up schoolgirl Japanese? You want to … *sex* with us?"

"Oh God, Yes!" I panted.

"You bring money?"

Of course, at that moment, I would have been willing to give her the deeds to my house, if only she would give me a long, loving kiss in return. But to my bank manager's eternal relief, once she'd seen all of my cash and credit cards, the schoolgirl took me by the hand and then led me inside the club.

"Don't worry." She giggled happily. "We all 18 and more."

I was almost literally in heaven. Everywhere I looked in this club, women of all races and nationalities were kissing and fucking gorgeous Japanese lesbians in full school uniform. Sexy young waitresses in full school uniform were delivering drinks, and even joining in with these Lesbian-Olympics. And up on stage, the '*Britney Spears*'-style plastic pop that I'd always despised, now that it was being performed by half a dozen gorgeous Oriental temptresses in a language that always made me cum, was now the most beautiful thing I'd ever heard.

"We sit and kiss?" Asked the adult schoolgirl, inviting me to that which I had always longed to do. And the next thing I knew we were both wrapped up in each other's embrace, kissing and caressing each other so deeply that my whole body began to tingle and I could barely breathe.

"You like white panties?" She teased maliciously, spreading her legs a little and licking her lips as she waited for me to stroke her pussy. "You want to touch?"

But although I wanted to reply, my hunger was so desperate that, before I even realised it, I was down on my knees with my head between the schoolgirl's legs, making her coo with ecstasy as I kissed and lapped at her soft, smooth, cotton-covered pussy. And as she gently slipped the knickers down around her ankles to reveal her wet, naked slit, I buried my tongue so deep inside her that it was her turn to shudder with delight.

I honestly couldn't tell you how long I spent licking that gorgeous schoolgirl's pussy. But by the time that my tongue was too exhausted to carry on, she had cum at least a half a dozen times. And, far to horny to care about the money, she begged me to let her lick my pussy as well.

Climbing back up onto the leather settee and slipping off my black satin knickers as the schoolgirl took my place down on her knees, I spread my legs and groaned with ecstasy, petting the grown-up schoolgirl's soft raven hair as she greedily licked every inch of my pussy and gobbled up the honey as it poured out of my slit. And a few moments later, when a sexy little waitress skipped over to ask if I wanted a drink, it wasn't long before I was kissing her to the point of breathlessness as I fingered her smooth, shaven slit.

Of course, no matter how much I might have wanted it, it would have been impossible for me to carry on fucking for the rest of my natural life. And so after a while, I had no choice but to stop for a short but well-earned break.

"Is this your first time?" Asked one of the other guests in a surprisingly familiar accent as I slowly made my way up to the bar to order a Bacardi and Coke. But still feeling too worn out from my sexual escapade to even catch my breath, although I wanted to start a conversation, I couldn't really do much apart from nod.

"Well, it's great to see that you're really getting stuck in and having a whale of a time."

But of course, the night was still young. And even if it wasn't, there were still more than a dozen other gorgeous schoolgirls to fuck until I lost all feeling in my tongue. And since the club had plenty of vacant rooms where the guests could either sleep, have a shower or '*get to know*' one of the girls more intimately, I honestly have no idea how long I spent there, gorging myself on sweet Oriental pussy until I literally saw stars.

The girls were even willing to buy anything that I wanted, for a modest fee of course, from a clean change of clothes to a strap on dildo. And so although it was daytime when I finally settled my bill and asked one of the girls to call for a taxi to take me back to the airport, I honestly had no idea what day of the week it actually was.

"You want … take thing with you?" Asked one of the girls, holding up the various dildos and sex toys that I'd made excellent use of over the course of my visit.

"No thank you." I smiled in reply. "Please keep them safe for my next visit."

And as I climbed into the taxi, drove out to the airport and boarded the first plane home, the only thought on my mind was how to make enough money to be able to go back.

The thought of going another six months without tasting sweet, delicious Japanese pussy was so heart-breaking that I didn't even dare to think about it, but by some spectacular coincidence, it seemed as though the fates had decided not to let me suffer for that long.

"Konichiwa," greeted a familiar voice as I kicked back in my seat.

I couldn't believe it. The gorgeous Japanese Schoolgirl who had been so worried about me on my first flight was now sitting only a few rows behind me. And despite having watched me wank in the toilet like a horny bitch on heat, she was still more than willing to come over and say hello.

"Konichiwa," I replied, trying to keep myself from cumming and speaking as calmly as I could.

"You … go back England?"

"Yes."

"I go back England too." She explained excitedly, making me so happy that I almost wanted to cry. "I go Japan for twenty-one birthday, but live London to learn

English. You live London too?"

"Yes! Yes I do!" I panted, completely unable to contain my excitement at the thought that she might live close to me.

"You … like girls?" She giggled mischievously, blushing with anticipation speaking very softly so as not to be overheard by anyone else.

"Yes. I *love* girls, and I love Japanese girls most of all."

"Is that why you … *play* yourself when you see me?"

And although I nodded, it was becoming clear that I didn't really need to reply.

"I like girls too." She whispered. "You want come and … play sex me as well?"

Kaz In The Changing Room
by Eleanor Powell

Kaz was looking for a new dress to wear at her cousin Rachel's twenty-first birthday party.

In Annabella's Boutique, she found two dresses that she thought would look good on her, but which one should she choose?

A helpful assistant, seeing Kaz dithering, came over.

'Can I help you, Madam?'

'Oh thanks,' I can't make up my mind which dress I like best.'

'Why don't you try them both on Madam? The changing room is this way.' She ushered Kaz into a large communal changing room.

'I'm sorry, Madam, but all the individual cubicles are in use,' she explained. 'But as you can see, at the moment there is no one else here.'

'Thank you,' said Kaz.

Stepping out of the dress she was wearing, she took the red dress off its hanger and slipped it over her head.

Looking at the reflection of this pretty girl, staring back at her in the full-length mirror, she could hardly believe it was herself. Her long shiny black hair cascaded over her shoulders.

She twirled one way, and then the other, noticing the

way the dress fell neatly over her slender hips, while her 'DD' sized boobs were showing a deep shadowy cleavage.

'I'd better try on the other dress,' she said aloud.

'Sweetheart, that dress is so right for you.' She hadn't noticed that she was no longer alone.

She jumped. 'I-I'm sorry,' she stammered, 'you gave me such a fright.'

She took in the appearance of the other occupant of the changing room. A tall girl, probably about six foot, not fat, but she had solid muscle.

She looked a bit out of place in Annabella's Boutique, as she was wearing a pair of faded blue jeans, a bomber jacket that was open, revealing a sloppy T-shirt under it. On her large feet, she was wearing a pair of trainers. Her auburn hair was cut very short, while her green eyes were shaded by the longest and thickest eyelashes Kaz had ever seen. She was blatantly looking Kaz up and down, admiringly.

'No it's me that should be apologising. I'm always being told to stop creeping up on people.'

'OK, don't worry,' said Kaz. 'So you really think this red dress looks all right, do you?'

'Yes, love, red suits you'

She stood behind Kaz. Touching her gently on her shoulder – receiving no resistance, she moved her finger, tracing her jaw line, down to her neck, then, slowly she trailed her finger down Kaz's cleavage. By now, Kaz felt her pussy juicing up. She was afraid to move in case the stranger stopped what she was doing.

Hesitantly, the stranger carried on. The fingers of her left hand found their way into Kaz's bra. She cupped the firm, large breast in her big hand, softly squeezing and kneading the fleshy breast. Pulling it out of its bra altogether, she fondled the pert nipples that had hardened and were sticking out like organ stops. Getting no objection from Kaz she pulled out her right breast, manipulating that nipple until it too was standing to attention.

Kaz was feeling so turned on. She had never felt this way before. Her head was thrown back, her deep blue eyes were closed and she was thrusting her tits forward, to make it as easy as possible for the other girl to get to her.

The stranger was now kissing the back of her neck. With her big strong hands, she turned Kaz round so they were facing each other.

Bending her head, she placed her mouth over Kaz's right tit, taking the stiffened nipple into her mouth. Gently she sucked on it, pulling on it, until it became elongated. Moving her mouth across to the left nipple, she sucked on it until it matched the right one.

She then let her hand wander down Kaz's flat belly, her fingers reached Kaz's Mound of Venus, and her big hand covered it.

Kaz gasped. Her pussy was throbbing and she knew the crutch of her knickers was getting soaked with her juices.

'Shall I carry on?' the stranger said in her ear.

'Please don't stop,' Kaz whispered.

Gently pushing Kaz against the wall, the stranger went down on her knees. She slid her hands up Kaz's hips, hooking her fingers into the waistband of her knickers; she rolled them down until they were at her ankles.

'Come on, Sweetheart, step out of them.' She nudged Kaz's legs apart, revealing the thick thatch of black hair and with her probing finger she found her engorged and throbbing clit and began to stroke it gently.

She replaced her finger with her tongue and began sucking on the wet swollen and squishy clit.

Kaz had a buzzing in her ears. She felt her whole pussy tingling and, oh, how she wanted this feeling to carry on for ever.

'My God, you're so wet,' said the stranger, going back to sucking Kaz's clit.

Kaz was finding it difficult to stay upright and she began to sag.

Noticing this, the stranger withdrew her finger from Kaz's steaming slit and said, 'Lie down, Sweetheart.' She helped her to lie on the carpeted floor of the changing room Taking off her jacket, she rolled it up and placed it under Kaz's head as a pillow.

Then kneeling beside Kaz, she cupped her face between her hands and put her mouth over Kaz's, her tongue exploring her mouth, Kaz could taste herself on the stranger's tongue.

Taking her tongue out of Kaz's mouth – she left a wet trail behind her as she moved her tongue down her body – causing Kaz to gasp and wriggle, as her whole body seemed to come alive and tingled.

'Are you enjoying this, Sweetheart?' the stranger asked.

'Yes, oh yes,'

'Great, so am I.' She again gave her full attention to Kaz's throbbing pussy.

Putting her finger into the wet interior she again began to rub the pulsating clit, gently at first, speeding up, as Kaz's muscles started squeezing on her finger.

'I-I'm going to come,' Kaz said.

The stranger while still strumming on Kaz's clit had put a finger into Kaz's pleasure hole, moving it in and out.

'Cum for me, Sweetheart,' said the stranger.

The buzzing in Kaz's ears became louder, and the tingling in her pussy spread to other parts of her body. It came in waves, ebbing and flowing. She was pushing down on the finger, squeezing it with her strong vaginal muscles.

Meanwhile, the stranger went back to using her tongue, licking up and down Kaz's inner thighs.

At last, Kaz came, moaning softly, her whole body shuddering.

'What is the meaning of this?' the shop assistant had come into the changing room, unnoticed by both Kaz and the stranger.

Kaz jumped to her feet, trying to smooth down the crumpled red dress in order to hide her bare bottom.

The stranger, who was still fully dressed, snatched up her jacket, mumbled an apology and left the changing room.

'Right, young lady, you have some explaining to do, haven't you?'

Kaz hung her head.

'I suggest,' said the shop assistant, 'that you agree that you have been a naughty girl and must be punished.'

'Punished, what do you mean?'

'I'm going to give you a spanking.' The shop assistant fetched a straight-backed chair, which was next to the open door and placed it in the middle of the room.

'Y-you can't do that to me,' Kaz backed away.

'Okay, in that case, I'll take you to see the manager. Look at the state that dress is in, we can't sell it now.'

'I'm sorry, please don't tell the manager.'

'Well it's either a spanking or the manager. Which is it to be?

'The-the spanking.'

'Then a spanking it shall be. I'll just lock the door so we won't be disturbed.'

Then sitting down on the chair, she pulled up her skirt and beckoned Kaz over to her side.

'Over my knee young lady.'

Kaz lowered her body over the other woman's naked thighs. Immediately the red dress was raised, clear of her bare backside. 'You have such a lovely bottom,' said the shop assistant, rubbing her hands over the quivering cheeks – spread out before her.

Lifting her right hand, she brought it down on Kaz's right cheek, quickly followed by her hand descending on her left cheek.

'Yeowww!' shrieked Kaz, wriggling about, trying to escape the stinging hand.

Despite Kaz's writhing and squirming about over her knee, the shop assistant's hard hand kept making contact with her ever-reddening bottom.

She only stopped spanking Kaz when she had covered the whole of her bottom, turning it as red as the crushed dress she was wearing.

Kaz lay limply over her assailant's knee – all the fight had gone out of her. The salty tears were running into the corners of her mouth.

Then the hand that had been spanking her so hard such short a time ago, was now, gently caressing her red hot stinging cheeks.

The shop assistant's fingers were exploring Kaz's innermost slit, stroking her clit momentarily, then continuing their exploration. Parting her bottom cheeks, she ran her finger up and down the crack, stopping to circle around her bottom hole. Then back down into Kaz's pussy. She went back to stroking the engorged clit with her right hand, making it throb even more. Putting her left index finger into Kaz's love passage she finger-fucked the young girl, causing her to buck over her knee.

For the second time, Kaz felt the waves of her orgasm overcoming her again as she climaxed – shuddering and shaking over the older woman's knee. She went limp once it was all over.

Helping Kaz to her feet, the shop assistant stood up. She removed her own knickers and sitting down again, she pulled her own skirt up and ordered Kaz to kiss her pussy. 'If you refuse,' she said, 'I can still take you to see the manager.'

Kaz quickly got down on her knees and, remembering what the stranger had done to her, she did the same to the shop assistant. Her inexperienced tongue found the other woman's clit and she began to suck and lick it.

'That feels so good.' The shop assistant put her hand on Kaz's head, forcing her to keep on eating her pussy.

Her body started to thrash about, she was coming, her juices tasted salty and Kaz found herself having to swallow quickly or she might have choked on them.

After a few moments, the shop assistant stood up, adjusting her dress.

She suggested Kaz also made herself presentable.

Kaz took off the red dress and put on the dress she'd been wearing when she first came into the shop.

'I'll wrap the dress for you,' said the shop assistant, folding the dress neatly and putting it into a plastic carrier bag, she handed it to Kaz.

'How much is it?' Kaz reached into her handbag for her purse.

The shop assistant smiled, 'You have more than paid for it, I hope you enjoy wearing it.'

'Thank you,' Kaz murmured. 'Bye bye.

'Thank you, madam, for shopping at Annabella's

Boutique. You have made a very wise choice,' she said. 'I hope you will come back again soon.'

Outside, the shop, the stranger was waiting for her and asked her, 'Did it work?'

'Of course it did,' she answered. 'Mind you, that was quite a spanking she gave me, but it was worth it.'

'Next week we'll try another shop, ' said the stranger.

Linking arms with each other, they headed for home.

Lessons Learned
by Lynn Lake

A couple of weeks ago, I hooked up with my friend Josee at the college she was attending. After she gave me a tour of the sprawling campus, we headed back to her dorm room to get ready for dinner – my treat. I hadn't seen Josee since high school graduation, as I had elected to attend an out-of-state college, but she hadn't changed any; she was still the same sleek, dark beauty she had always been. Her breasts were high and firm – not too big, not too small – and her skin was smooth and pale, her delicate face framed by shoulder-length coal-black hair. She was shy and a little awkward, but she had a warm smile and a look that said 'still waters run deep'.

"So, what do you think, Marie? You going to transfer?" she asked, unlocking the door to her dorm room and letting me inside.

"Well, I don't know," I said, playing it coy. "What's the after-class atmosphere like around here? You know, the party scene?"

She blushed, put her keys down on a small wooden desk, and then perched on the edge of one of the two beds in the tiny room. "I thought you said you were finally going to get serious about your studies?"

I sat on the other bed, facing her. I studied her dark

eyes, her full, red lips. She had a pair of faded blue jeans on and a white T-shirt, and I could smell the sweet body spray that she was wearing. "Oh, I intend to get serious," I told her.

There followed a long and awkward silence during which I stared openly at her, at her face and body, the burning lust in my eyes sending out flaming tendrils that desperately sought to spark her own desire. I'd known Josee since junior high, but only recently had I realised that my feelings for her had become more than just friendly. An easy-going, big-breasted blonde like myself had no trouble attracting the guys, but it was girl-love I was after, now – with my best girl.

I shifted positions, sat down next to her, and placed my left hand on her leg, up around her thigh. Upon contact with her hot, hard body, my nipples instantly grew erect under my thin halter top, and my pussy was consumed with so much heat and moisture that I thought I'd soak my cut-off jeans. "You must get lonely without me around?" I whispered, my voice breaking. I blatantly squeezed her leg, then let my hand drift higher, up around her hip.

She turned beet-red. She glanced at my hand, swallowed hard, and croaked, "It's, uh, not so bad. I … have a roommate. She's supposed to be –"

I halted her foolish prattle by moving my bold hand over the top of her crotch. I began rubbing her there, softly yet urgently rubbing her. I'd waited so long, masturbated so many times to the mental image of she and I ravaging each other with the pent-up fury of secret lovers, and I was determined to make up for lost time.

I said, "Your roommate doesn't do this, I bet," breathing into her innocent face, reaching out with my right hand and touching her neck with my fingers. I

160

caressed the delicate, ivory skin on the side of her throat, then my fingers wandered across her shoulder, down her back, and up and under her T-shirt. I kept rubbing her pussy through the thin fabric of her jeans, as I pulled her shirt out of her pants and slid my hand underneath and began stroking her bare skin.

"Marie, I'm … not sure …"

Her words caught in her throat when I popped open her bra and bent closer to kiss her on the cheek. I pressed home my advantage by pushing her down onto the bed, until she was flat on her back and I was on top of her. "I've wanted this for so long," I murmured, grasping her shoulders and kissing her gently on her soft, soft lips.

"Oh," she exclaimed, startled by my overpowering craving for her.

I peeled off my top, exposing my large, heavy breasts to her wonder-struck eyes. My nipples were thick and long – chocolate-brown compared to the rest of my sun-burnished upper body. I kissed her again, but this time I lingered. I pressed my lips hard against hers, covered her mouth with mine, began to consume her. My tongue darted out and painted her pouty lips with hot saliva.

She mumbled something about slowing down, but I swallowed her protests. I attacked her mouth, ploughing my tongue up against her teeth, forcing my way inside. I hungrily explored the soft, moist interior of her mouth, swirling my tongue around, trying to engage her own tongue, my damp hands gripping the sides of her head, my fingers buried in the shimmering black curtain of her hair. I devoured her sweet goodness, kissing hard and long and openly, waiting impatiently, desperately for her to respond, until, finally, I felt her hands cover my bare breasts! She gently caressed and squeezed my big tits. My body flooded with pure, blinding joy and my head spun.

I gazed into her half-frightened, half-lusty eyes. "I'm going to make love to you, Josee," I said.

"Please," she murmured.

I kissed her, and this time my yearning tongue was met by her tongue. We slapped our tongues against one another, and I moaned into her open mouth when she pulled on my rock-hard nipples. My body tingled with the sensual sensation of her eager, shaking hands. Her tongue snaked out and I caught it between my teeth. I sucked on her tongue, sucked up and down its slippery length like it was a hardened cock. Then I kissed her neck, licked her neck, bit her neck, kissed and licked behind her delicate ears.

Her super-heated body fired my raging desire into an inferno. "Take off your clothes," I moaned into her ear, then swirled my thick tongue around inside of it.

"Yes," she anxiously agreed. "Yes."

I released my sexual convert, and she scrambled up off the bed and tore off her T-shirt and pulled down her jeans. She fumbled her shoes away and stepped out of her jeans and stood in front of me, naked except for her girlish, white, cotton panties. Her over-wrought body trembled as my eyes drank in her sculptured, porcelain beauty. Her breasts were beautifully shaped, milky globes peaked by inch-long, impossibly-pink nipples. Her stomach was flat and hard, her waist narrow, her hips round and firm.

She smiled nervously and reached for her panties, but my hands shot out and stopped her. "Let me," I said, licking my swollen lips. I stood and slowly stripped off my shoes and shorts and panties. Her eyes flashed fire as she beheld my nude, over-ripe body. I cupped my huge, bronze breasts and spread my legs, and she stared in awe at my shaved, glistening pussy. My pink folds were wet and raw with wanting.

"Fuck me, Marie!" she hissed, unable to control herself any longer.

I knelt down in front of her, as Roman she-warriors once knelt down before the goddess Venus, and I groped the full roundness of her firm buttocks. I squeezed her taut ass cheeks, fondling their splendid shape with my worshipping hands. Then I grasped the sides of her panties and tugged them down, leaving them puddled at her feet. She lifted her long, slender legs and stepped out of the discarded undergarment, and I gazed hungrily at her slickened slit. She, too, was shaved for maximum pleasure, except for a small tuft of soft, black fur that crowned her juicy pussy.

I lashed out my tongue and slashed at her cunny. She shuddered with the impact. I teased her pussy with my tongue, then lifted her right leg off the floor and placed her foot on the bed. Now I had unrestricted access to her gaping, glistening cunt. I lapped at her moistened folds ferociously, forced my pointed tongue into and through her plump, pink pussy lips. I spread her wider with my fingers and buried my tongue inside her twat, joyously tasting her hot lovejuices for the very first time. I slammed my tongue in and out of her, fucking her with my slimy pleasure tool like it was a swollen cock.

"Yes!" she cried, frantically squeezing and kneading her pert tits, viciously pulling and rolling her engorged nipples, her tawny body quivering with the sexual shockwaves that my talented tongue was generating within her molten pussy.

I lapped at her cunny like a kitten laps at a saucer of warm milk, revelling in the taste of her. Then I ploughed two fingers into her steaming lovebox and began fervently finger-fucking her as I teased her clit with my tongue. My fingers flew in and out of her tight pussy, driving her wild, driving me wild.

"I'm going to come, Marie!" she screamed. Her face was contorted into a grim mask of barely contained ecstasy, and tears of lust trailed down her flaming cheeks and into her open mouth. She let go of her titties and grabbed my head, tore at my hair, desperately clinging to me as her body was inundated with red-hot lesbian passion.

I pulled my fingers out of her soaking wet pussy, carefully licked off her juices, and then spread her wide and sucked hard on her clit. I was anxious to have my greedy mouth flooded by her impending orgasm.

"Fuck, yes!" she yelled out, oblivious to the other residents of the thin-walled dorm. Her slim body was jolted by orgasm. Muscles contracted up and down her exquisite torso, and she spasmed over and over and over, her tits jouncing up and down as she was torn asunder by white-hot ecstasy that centred on her pussy and my mouth.

I frenziedly sucked on her clit, and was quickly drenched with the liquid fruits of my labour of love – an orgasmic release of a tidal wave of fiery girl-juice. She came on my face, in my mouth, her hips bucking, her butt cheeks shuddering, her mouth opening and closing with silent screams of total abandon. I drank in as much of her womanly goodness as I could. I swallowed and swallowed her cum as she was devastated by multiple orgasms.

"Jesus," she finally gasped, her tits trembling with the aftershocks of volcanic release, her body sheathed in dewy perspiration.

I licked up and down her pussy, slurping up the last

few drops of her tangy cum, and then nipped at her clit in a parting salute. I looked up at her and grinned, my lips and chin shiny with her honey. "Now it's my turn," I said.

"Sure," she agreed, sounding exhausted. "Why don't-"

We were suddenly interrupted by the door popping open. We whipped our heads around and stared at the intruder, a young woman. If she was surprised by the spectacular sight of two naked, nubile girls, one kneeling at the drenched pussy of the other, she didn't show it.

"Hi, Taylor," Josee said easily.

I glanced at her in surprise, at the mischievous smile playing across her puffy lips.

"Hi, Josee," the girl called Taylor replied, closing the door securely behind her. "Looks like your plan worked, after all."

Josee shrugged her shoulders, smoothed my hair down. "Well, actually, it turned out that Marie had a plan of her own. I just sorta played along."

Taylor advanced into the room as I scrambled to my feet. "Nice to meet you, Marie," she said. "I'm Josee's roommate. She's told me a lot about you." She reached out and shook my hand, which seemed a strange thing to do to a naked woman, but she topped that by kissing her roommate squarely on the lips. They frenched each other familiarly as I gaped in amazement. My shy, innocent Josee obviously wasn't nearly as shy nor innocent as she had led me to believe.

"Are you and Josee … lovers?" I asked Taylor in disbelief, when the two girls had finally ceased their tongue-wrestling.

"Every chance we get," the young woman replied, laughing. "Right, Jo?"

Josee nodded. "But we've never had a threesome

before. You up for it, Marie?"

"Oh, I think she's up for it, all right," Taylor replied for me, reaching out to fondle my swollen nipples – the exclamation points on my mounting excitement.

I looked at Josee, and she grinned back at me and fingered her pussy. "Uh, I-I …" I stuttered, then gave up as my body was suffused with the erotic heat of Taylor's tit-groping. She really knew her way around a girl's mammaries.

"Mmmm," I moaned, as Taylor squeezed my big tits together and rolled my nipples. I regarded her through lowered eyelids and saw that she was built along the same lines that I was – big and curvaceous. She had long, wavy, auburn hair, and her large eyes were warm and brown, her chest huge and heaving. She was barely wearing a red tube-top and black spandex pants. I closed my eyes for a moment, basking in the warm feel of her hands on my tits, and then, when I re-opened my eyes, Taylor was wearing nothing at all. And now Josee was the one fondling my tits, firing my pussy.

"Now, how shall we do this?" Taylor pondered, bouncing a finger on her puckered lips. "Oh, I know. Josee can eat out Marie's pussy, while Marie gives me a little of what she gave Josee. Sound fair?"

We both nodded. When the positioning had been hastily completed, the erotic entanglement left me lying on my back on one of the beds, Josee's head between my legs, with Taylor balanced just above me, facing the wall, her knees on either side of my face. I quickly grabbed onto Taylor's plump, round buttocks and pulled her soaking snatch down into my mouth.

"Yeah," she moaned. "Do me like you did Josee."

I lapped at Taylor's cunny and massaged her beautiful behind. She tasted as good as Josee, and I couldn't get enough. Meanwhile, Josee was driving me wild by licking my pussy with the polished, frenetic skill of a dedicated muff-diver. I moaned into Taylor's cunt and the girl's body quivered with the vibrations of my voice.

Josee reached up and played with my titties while she kindled my cunt-fire with her tongue. She squeezed my breasts and sucked on my clit, making me dizzy with her sexual skills, and it was all I could do to keep on tongue-lashing Taylor's luscious snatch. I licked up and down her pussy, over and over, then around and into her ass. She jumped when my wet, probing tongue explored her tiny bunghole.

"What a fantastic sight," Josee said, momentarily raising her head from my shiny womanhood to gaze at the sexy scenario of her pretty roommate climbing the wall as I furiously lapped at her pussy and ass.

"Fuck almighty, I'm coming!" Taylor cried out, cutting short the time for introspection.

Josee dipped her talented tongue back into my pussy and re-doubled her efforts, trying to bring me off in sync to Taylor's mounting orgasm. I clenched Taylor's butt and drove my tongue deep into the quaking girl's cunny. Josee was sucking hard on my clit, and my head started to spin as my senses were overwhelmed with the smell and taste of Taylor's molten womanhood and the sensuous sensation of Josee's cunt-licking.

"Here I come!" Taylor shrieked.

Her butt cheeks jumped around in my hands as her perfect body was wracked by a tongue-inspired orgasm. I frantically clung to her pussy with my mouth, drinking down her liquid ecstasy as she came over and over again. Then, before Taylor had ceased her gyrations of joy, my own body blazed with fire and my mind was sent reeling. Josee's cuntwork had pushed me over the edge. I shut my eyes and clung to Taylor's bucking rump as the tingling in my pussy exploded into electric shocks that jolted my body like I'd been plugged into a wall socket. My pussy erupted and I drenched Josee's sweet face with my lovejuices.

"Yeah!" I screamed, shattered by thundering orgasms that detonated inside of me and wasted my body and mind. I gasped for air, found only pussy, and my ecstasy was like nothing I had ever experienced before.

Taylor dropped down onto my stomach and covered my gaping mouth with her own, swallowing my cries of pleasure, as Josee continued to relentlessly tongue-fuck me and polish my clit with her thumb. I thought I was headed for blackout when a final orgasm, the most powerful one yet, tore through my body and into Taylor's sucking mouth. Then I lay shaken and dazed in the afterglow of total fulfilment, my body dappled with sweat, my soul obliterated.

Josee crawled up behind Taylor, encircled the girl's tits with her arms, and the two girlfriends shared my cum with each other, swapping it back and forth with their tongues. I watched through a thick, warm haze, my body languid, my brain struggling to regain a foothold on reality.

"Do you think Marie's going to transfer, now?" Josee asked Taylor, as the devious scamp felt up Taylor's big tits and pointed nipples.

They looked at me.

"I don't know," Taylor replied. "I think she still needs some more convincing."

I smiled weakly, willing to learn all I could.

The Education Of Clarissa
by Izzy French

"Oh, Sylvia, darling, it was just horrid." Clarissa threw her suitcase across the room and fell onto the bed, in her usual dramatic fashion. Sylvia remained silent; there was little need to speak. Clarissa would not be able to resist the telling of her tale. Sylvia listened to her sigh and watched her pass the back of her hand across her eyes and draw her knees up.

"Truly horrid. Too awful to tell. Come over here, please won't you, sweetheart? Offer me some shred of comfort in my hour of need."

Sylvia had no doubt that Clarissa would end up on the stage. She went and knelt beside her friend and roommate, taking her proffered hand. She stroked it softly. Her friend's fingers were long and slim, her skin as soft as silk.

"Poor you," she soothed. "Why don't you just lie back and tell me all about it."

Clarissa had just returned from a weekend home, an unusual occurrence for boarders during term time at St Hilda's. But it had been a special occasion, for which Clarissa's father had sought permission well in advance, her parents' twenty-fifth wedding anniversary. And, as sixth-formers, they were entitled to special dispensations, sometimes. The party was to be fabulous. Clarissa's family were landed, owning a rambling Tudor mansion in the country. Clarissa's dress had been made by the finest Parisian couturier, from beautiful peacock-blue satin. And, in addition to the overall grandeur of the event, Clarissa also planned for it to be a special occasion personally. She intended to lose her virginity. She had informed Sylvia of this moments before leaving on Friday evening.

"But it's top secret of course," she'd added in one of her stage whispers. "I want to know a man, to touch him, before my parents marry me off to some hideous cousin and it all comes as some horrible surprise on my wedding night. I want to it experience it now. With someone young and beautiful. Don't you ever feel that need?"

Sylvia didn't reply. She wasn't sure she did. Not in the way Clarissa described. At night, sometimes, she explored the curves and crevices of her own body, experienced a brief but sweet sensation as she felt between her thighs. But that was the problem. She enjoyed the feel of her own body, and thought about the bodies of other girls when she was doing so. Not boys or men. The thought of them repulsed her. Though she had never shared this with Clarissa.

Sylvia had respected her friend's confidentiality, but had spent the whole weekend dying to know what had happened. Clarissa had even decided who the lucky recipient of her virginity would be – Archie, the son of one of her father's closest friends. Charles, Clarissa's brother, Archie and Clarissa, had virtually grown up together.

"He's so handsome, now, Sylvia, just like James Dean," she'd said. So the last thing Sylvia had been expecting was for Clarissa to declare her deflowering as being horrid. A little painful, maybe, or messy. But not horrid.

"Wasn't Archie gentle?" she ventured.

"Archie? Oh, Lord, I have lots to tell about Archie. And Charles too. It soon became apparent that it wouldn't be Archie making love to me. Why would he, when he was doing that exact thing with Charles?"

Sylvia gasped, as she was sure she was expected to.

"Yes, I came across them in the summer house together. Both entirely naked and entangled. They saw me, but didn't even part, so I ran back towards the house and bumped into him on the way."

"Him?"

"Oh, yes, haven't I said? It all finally happened with Lord Shrewsbury."

"But isn't he ...?"

"Old? Yes. Thirty-five at least. Oh, and married too of course. But then she's a shrew, so who can blame him for straying?"

Who, indeed, thought Sylvia, looking at her friend lying on the bed, her thick dark hair falling over the pillow, her lips plump and moist, her brown eyes turned to her. Sylvia reached forward and stroked Clarissa's hair, hoping to coax out more of the tale, and to be able to offer solace if it was required.

"He was a savage, Sylvia, darling, all hard and hairy and thrusting. And it was over so quickly. All I was left with was a tear in my gown and a bruise on my back where I'd been leaning on the wall of the pagoda."

She reached out and touched Sylvia's cheek in return.

"Even his lips were hard and rough. Not like your sweet lips." Clarissa ran her forefinger over Sylvia's mouth. "I'm giving up on men. Come up here and kiss me. I need comforting."

Sylvia obeyed Clarissa's instruction, almost kissing her on the cheek, but at the last moment Clarissa's mouth met her lips. For a moment they were still. The warmth of Clarissa's lips on her own made Sylvia melt, then she felt her friend's lips part, and they began to move together, their kiss becoming insistent and firm, until Clarissa broke away moments later.

"Oh, God, I'm so sorry," Sylvia felt her whole body flush with heat, she stood and headed for the door. Clarissa caught her hand and pulled her onto the bed.

"Don't say sorry. It was me. I've been dying to know how your lips would taste compared to his. They're so sweet. He tasted of whisky and tobacco. You taste of violets. Kiss me again."

Sylvia hesitated. Was this a trap? She turned to Clarissa. Her eyes were open wide, and they held her gaze, refusing to let her wander.

"I insist you kiss me again."

Clarissa's aristocratic tones brooked no argument. She was lying back on the pillow, her arms above her head. Sylvia lay on the bed next to her, reached over and kissed her. The second kiss was sweeter still, more prolonged and certain. Sylvia sensed they both knew that this felt right. Her body was aching now, with need and desire. Would the kiss be it? It was High Tea soon. Would they break away, go down to the hall together, enjoy sandwiches and scones, and never speak of these moments again? Just then the bell rang. They were due in the hall within minutes. They froze, still kissing, the tip of Clarissa's tongue resting between Sylvia's teeth. The bell ceased ringing. They resumed their kiss. Clarissa placed her hands around Sylvia's cheeks, cupping them. She finally pulled away, though Sylvia knew then that this would not finish now. Clarissa caressed her cheeks with the tips of her fingers.

"Your skin's so soft. Why would any girl wish to kiss a man who could scratch her face to pieces, when she could kiss you?"

Sylvia didn't know the answer to that, but was happy to accept that, for now, it was Clarissa's wish. She wanted to hold her friend now, tight, to feel her skin against her own, but she held back, wanting Clarissa to take the lead.

"I want more of you." Clarissa whispered.

"And I want more of you too," smiled Sylvia, relieved and happy.

They turned to face one another and kissed again. Sylvia felt Clarissa's hand run down her side and pull her pinafore above her hip. The stroke of her hand on her thigh sent a shiver to her centre.

"I want to feel and see all of you," Clarissa said. "I saw so little of him. Just his cock and the tops of his hairy thighs. Making love should be about the whole person, surely? Like it was with Charles and Archie. They were giving everything to each other. I could tell that, and that it wasn't the first time they had either. I'm sure of that too."

"I want that to feel what they were feeling." Sylvia was feeling bolder. She began to unbutton Clarissa's pale blue silk blouse, a little embarrassed at her own regulation navy serge pinafore and thick lisle stockings. Not like the delicate nylons that Clarissa wore, held up with a pretty suspender belt, no doubt. Once the blouse was open she pushed it back from Clarissa's shoulders and gazed at her breasts encased in the pale pink satin bra. Clarissa shrugged the blouse away and threw it to the floor.

"We'll be the same when we're naked," Clarissa

173

reassured, obviously reading Sylvia's discomfort. "But there's no rush."

Clarissa tucked her fingers under the tops of Sylvia's stockings, causing Sylvia to groan with pleasure, at the sensation of her friend's touch. She pressed her thighs together, feeling the familiar wetness. But this feeling was so much more intense, so sweet. She pushed Clarissa's bra straps off her shoulders, and kissed the tops of her breasts. She wanted to feel her nipples between her lips, to suck and bite them, to squeeze them between her fingertips.

"Shall I take it off?" Clarissa anticipated her need.

Sylvia nodded.

"He couldn't have cared less about my breasts. Or my pleasure at all for that matter. I can see that you won't be so careless, Sylvia, darling."

Clarissa reached around her back and released the clasp of her brassiere, throwing it to the floor on top of her blouse. She fell back onto the bed, her firm, full breasts bouncing as she did so. Her nipples and areola were large and brown. Sylvia had to taste these beautiful buds. She leant forwards and took the right one between her lips, feeling it harden, as, at first, she licked it gently, then sucked more vigorously. Clarissa had begun to re-explore her thighs, reaching higher this time, pushing the flat of her hand against her mound, rubbing the rough fabric of her knickers, and pulling them up between her slit.

"You've got an advantage over me darling," Clarissa stated. "You're wearing more clothes. Take some off. Your knickers please. And that hideous girdle."

Sylvia flushed again at the ugliness of her school undergarments, rose to stand at the side of the bed with her back to Clarissa, and shrugged herself out of her stockings, knickers and girdle, allowing her pinafore to cover her nakedness.

"The dress and blouse too, of course."

Sylvia pulled her remaining clothes over her head and rejoined her friend on the bed.

"That's better, no obstacles this time," Clarissa smiled as she ran her hand from Sylvia's knee, up her thigh, and between her legs, exploring her folds with a firm but gentle touch. Sylvia felt her legs squeeze around Clarissa's hand involuntarily, and she gasped as her friend rolled her tiny nub of pleasure between her fingers. This felt so much better than her own rapid and silent explorations in the dead of night.

"You are so beautiful, Sylvia, darling."

"You, too." Sylvia had grown confident. She undid the button and zip on the back of Clarissa's skirt, and pushed it down over the curve of her hips. Her stomach was gently rounded and her French knickers matched her brassiere. The silk was of the finest quality, and Sylvia could see Clarissa's dark curls through the fabric. She pressed her hand against the darkness, and could feel the moistness of her desire though the fabric too.

"He made me take him in his mouth, you know. The first time. Before he fucked me. You'll taste sweeter, I know." Clarissa moved down the bed, resting her head first against Sylvia's stomach. Then she planted dozens of tiny kisses around her belly button. Kisses that sent shots of delicious desire to Sylvia's core.

"Your skin is as soft as butter, Sylvia," she whispered before reaching lower still, nuzzling her face in Sylvia's curls. "And you smell divine. Not like him. All cologne and sweat."

Clarissa bent her head again. This time her tongue parted Sylvia's folds, tasting her juices. Sylvia groaned with pleasure, a pleasure so much more divine than that achieved on her own. She parted her legs, allowing Clarissa access to her centre of bliss. She felt her tongue insinuate its way between her folds, exploring her, devouring her. This was beyond her wildest imaginings. She felt herself tighten, as if the waves of pleasure were about to unfold and rush over her, when Clarissa pulled away.

"You taste wonderful too, Sylvia." Her fingers had taken the place of her tongue, for now. They had found their way to her opening and were delving inside her, meeting little resistance, besides the tightening of desire.

"Charles said he and Archie pleasure each other together, sometimes. Shall we try?"

Before Sylvia had a chance to answer there was a knock at the door. The two girls froze.

"Clarissa? Sylvia? Are you in there?" They remained silent.

"You're late for evening prayer. Hurry now." Miss Bannister's voice was peremptory.

They glanced at one another and stifled a giggle. Miss Bannister's footsteps tapped away on the corridor.

They turned to one another.

"I'd like to try that thing that Charles and Archie do. Can we?" Now Sylvia was bold enough to try anything. Her pleasure, and that of Clarissa, was paramount, and urgent. Clarissa turned herself around on the tiny bed, legs straddling Sylvia, stomach to stomach, showing Sylvia the full beauty of her cunt. For a few moments Sylvia just looked, admiring the delicate moist folds surrounded by tight, dark curls.

"Aren't you going to touch?" Clarissa asked, before delving again between Sylvia's legs with a fervour that relighted her desire. At first she was lost in herself,

176

wanting her flame to be quenched, its intensity almost painful with the desire for fulfilment. Then the need to give pleasure to Clarissa overtook her, and she reached for her friend's hips and pulled her down to her mouth. The taste of her was exquisite. Creamy and warm, Clarissa's juices ran down her tongue, like nectar into a bee. Clarissa pushed against her, demonstrating her own pleasure. Rhythmically and silently they moved against one another, kissing, sucking, nibbling, driving each other towards fulfilment. Desire and friction raised their body heat. Sylvia matched Clarissa's moves. When a tongue encircled her clitoris, she ran hers around Clarissa's, knowing it was creating the desired effect by her friend's moans of pleasure. She plunged three fingers inside her in response to feeling herself opened up by her friend's hand; then tightened around it as her climax drew near. It was unstoppable now, and as Clarissa's cunt squeezed her own fingers faster, she knew hers was too. Sylvia cried out loud as her release finally came, and it was of an intensity she had only dreamed of. She could only focus on her cunt, at the heart of her being, as it radiated pleasure throughout her body. As her climax ebbed towards satisfaction Clarissa turned and reached up to kiss her, allowing Sylvia to taste the sweetness of her own juices. She knew from the glow and smile on her friend's face that she was fulfilled too.

"I like that thing Archie and Charles do, "Clarissa said, drawing Sylvia close, so they could lie in each other's arms, kissing and touching. They would be late too for evening prayers now.

Naseem
by N. Vasco

Its funny how something like dinner at a new restaurant with some friends can lead to big changes in your life but that's exactly what happened to me about a week ago.

To start with, I had immersed myself in work for almost a year after my divorce, my social life was practically non-existent and my sex life basically consisted of masturbating occasionally to an erotic book, magazine or some website I found particularly appealing.

Then, some of the girls at work invited me to a dinner at the new Middle-Eastern restaurant that had opened near the office. Since I had nothing planned, as usual, I said "yes", and went along, hearing them gripe about their husbands, boyfriends and children. Needless to say, I felt a little out of place when it came to domestic subjects but hearing how difficult it can be for single mothers, I was particularly glad my ex and I never started a family. I was all ready to enjoy my food while adding to the small talk circulating around the table when the lights dimmed and the strains of Middle-Eastern music filled the restaurant.

When the tempo increased, a heavily accented man announced the evening's entertainment. Just as the music switched to a hard driving beat a spotlight fell on a gorgeous, elegant, dark-haired belly dancer in the centre of the restaurant, her tawny body surrounded by tiny stars sparkling off her rhinestone halter and exotic jewellery.

She scanned the room with her dark eyes as the music got louder and then raised her arms before starting a hip-shaking dance, her brown body swaying and flowing in one of the most alluringly sexy performances I had seen in a long time.

Needless to say, I was mesmerized. Before long my throat felt constricted and dry despite the occasional sip of wine from the glass I clutched in my hands, my nipples itching like never before as a hot, wet sensation blossomed between my legs.

I caught the occasional comments from my girlfriends and nodded while trying not to stare at the dancer's moves and before long the heat radiating from my belly seemed to flow under every inch of my skin. When I rested my free hand on my thigh, allowing my warm palm to touch my bare flesh, I instantly felt like masturbating and wanted to be home, at the same time wishing the performance would never end.

Then, with a loud flourish of cymbals the music ended, the dancer's body was covered in a sheen as she struck a final, graceful pose; a slender ankle raised, her pointed toes barely touching the floor, the lovely curves of her bottom arched out, her heaving breasts rising with quick breaths. The spotlight went out for a couple of seconds as applause and cheers filled the now dark interior.

Needless to say as soon as I got home I stripped off my clothes and masturbated. Normally, I like to set things up. Soft music, candlelight, an erotic book or a sexy video and the collection of "toys" I own are always nice but that night was different. I found myself on my

179

back, ignoring the cold hardwood floor on my bare skin as I masturbated, remembering that sexy dancer until I lay exhausted and spent.

After a quick shower I slipped into a nice bubble bath, enjoying that sleepy afterglow and caressing myself. As I luxuriated in the warm tub I began to wonder why I was so turned on. The dancer was beautiful and yes, I had had my share of women in the past but this was completely different.

Then I remembered. My lips whispered a name I hadn't uttered in a long time: "Naseem".

It was during my last year in college when an incredibly sexy Iranian beauty moved into my dorm. Naseem was gregarious, beautiful and smart. She had this incredible, narrow-waisted figure she carried with a smooth elegance, her pearly skin, jet-black hair and huge, dark eyes reminding me of the beauties I read about in the Arabian Nights.

I did feel a strong attraction to Naseem but after we became friends I decided not to jeopardise our friendship, no matter how horny I got each time I saw her. She did have an active social life and at that time I was seeing the guy I would eventually marry (and later divorce), so nothing really started between us.

We used to borrow each other's clothes and one night when I was in her dorm room, looking through her closet, I heard her voice and another girl's out in the hallway. I don't know what possessed me to hide in the closet and watch what would happen next but that's exactly what I did.

Peering through a crack in the closet door I watched her and June, a pretty little Vietnamese girl with a deliciously curvaceous figure. I knew June from some of the classes we took together. Despite the attention a lot of guys paid to her sexy body, I never saw her out with anyone except Ann, a pretty, doll faced Filipina with a fantastic ass (someone once said she had the face of an angel and the body of a porn star) who was in an on-again, off-again relationship with her boyfriend.

Before the door even closed they instantly fell in each other's arms while undressing and exchanging deep, probing kisses until they were completely naked, June's pretty, brown body contrasting nicely with Naseem's pearly-skinned beauty.

By then I was already touching myself, my fingers toying with my hard nipples while my other hand pulled off my shorts so I could stroke my wet crotch and before I knew what I was doing I was naked and masturbating.

I watched June lick and suck on Naseem's big, brown nipples as the first hints of pleasure made my skin tingle but just then I saw Naseem get up and walk to the stereo she kept near her bed. I wondered what was going on until I heard this hard-driving Middle Eastern music just before Naseem began a very sexy belly dance. I had seen belly dancing on occasion and even got to watch Naseem perform during a cultural fair our Sorority held once but back then she wore a costume that covered her from head to foot.

This was nothing like that. I watched her dance and touched myself, occasionally glancing at June as she caressed her tawny curves. When the music ended they fell in a naked embrace, their arms and legs entwined around each other. Before I knew it, I grabbed the nearest thing hanging I could find (a scarf) and wadded it in my mouth as to stifle my orgasmic moans.

As my body shook and undulated with pleasure I watched them on the bed in a sixty-nine position, their heads between each other's thighs and after a while they came, their fingers inside each other's wet loins and pliant cheek holes, their orgasmic moans replacing the fading music.

By then the scarf in my mouth was wet with saliva, the warm, wet coat on my fingers chilling as I pulled up my shorts and tried to straighten out my blouse. I closed my eyes and wondered if I had to spend the night in the closet, even entertaining the notion about joining them but when I opened my eyes I saw they had propped some pillows against the headboard, and were just chatting.

Yes, I felt a little guilty, not only did I watch them making love but now I was hearing personal stuff like June's infatuation with Ann who at times seemed to be interested but couldn't bring herself to break up with the loser boyfriend who kept putting her down. I also got the impression they were more like friends who enjoyed an occasional lay instead of steady lovers and just as I was steeling my nerves and getting ready apologise for being such a voyeur I heard them talk about going out for coffee. After a few minutes they got dressed and left me sitting in the closet, Naseem's ruined scarf in my hand. The memory of that sexy encounter was tucked away in my memory until that night in the restaurant.

It wasn't hard to find out what happened to Naseem and where she was since we were Alumni from the same University. I found out she lived in Vegas, was a nurse in one of the upscale clinics just off the strip and danced in a Middle Eastern restaurant whose website included some very sexy pictures of her. It didn't take long for me to decide I needed a vacation and booked a flight to Vegas.

I had the concierge at my hotel make reservations at the restaurant Naseem danced in and at the last minute found a lovely silk scarf that closely resembled the one I ruined when I watched her and June make love.

When I got to the restaurant my heart was literally in my throat. I barely touched my food or wine and was beginning to have second thoughts when the lights dimmed and music began playing. Just then a black-haired dancer with an all-too-familiar body in diaphanous red silks, the gold bangles on her wrists and slender ankles reflecting the spotlight trailing her, floated into the centre of the restaurant and began writhing and undulating to the sexy, hard-driving music.

When she came near my table her black eyes smiled with recognition and made my heart skip a beat, my eyes glued to that pearly body weaving among the tables. After a couple more dances, one even performed with a curved scimitar balanced on her head, the music stopped just before she blew a few kisses to the audience applauding her excellent performance. Before she left she sought me out and gestured with her lovely, jewelled hands to wait until she came back.

I kept on touching the wrapped package containing the scarf, while occasionally nibbling at my food and taking the occasional sip of my drink. Before I knew it, Naseem was walking towards my table, wearing a tight, short little black cocktail dress hugging her excellent body, the gold bangles on her wrists and the delicate chains around her slender ankles adding to her exotic good looks.

We exchanged a brief kiss and she asked me how I was and before I knew it we were chatting away while exchanging the occasional, tender caress, our hands at times resting on each other's thighs. When her eyes fell on the package I told her it was a gift. She planted a quick yet electrifying kiss on my lips, her hand briefly resting on my thigh before opening her gift.

The kiss took me by surprise but when she held the

scarf in her elegant hands I was almost floored.

"I always wondered if you were ever going to replace the one you messed up."

"You knew?" I said, not knowing whether to laugh or feel embarrassed.

"Of course." She replied with a matter of fact tone, a seductive twinkle in her dark eyes. "I saw you enter my room. When June and I walked in I knew you were still there even though I didn't see you."

"Did June know?"

"I didn't want the situation to get awkward. That's why I put on some music and danced before we made love. To distract her in case you made any noises of your own."

She even went on to tell me that June and Ann finally got together after Ann broke up with her boyfriend.

"Are you angry with me for not telling you sooner?"

"Why should I be the angry one?" I replied. "I was the one who ruined your scarf."

We shared a good laugh while squeezing and caressing each other's thighs under the table, our legs around each other, her sexy high heels rubbing against my calf. When I suggested we go up to my room she responded with a cool, hooded smile.

Yes, we made love. Hot passionate love. Warm juicy sweet tender and rough, the taste of her mouth as sweet as the juices flowing out of her hot loins, her fingers alone doing things to me that I had never felt before. We actually started slowly at first, undressing each other as soon as the door closed behind us, our bodies pressed against each other, the contours of her curvaceous form fitting so nicely against mine as we slowly made our way to my bed.

She told me to lie down while I was still dressed, her

hands pushing up my hem and then pulling down the wet little nothing panties I wore that evening, her cooing voice telling me how lovely and sexy I looked and how nice I smelled. She played around my wet loins, her fingers strumming the soft area of my inner thighs, her teeth gently nibbling at my hot belly as I pulled off my dress before toying with my hard, itching nipples. When she rubbed my wet lips between her fingers, her darting tongue teasing my swollen clit, I was instantly seized by this juicy pleasure that rushed through my body that became even more intense when her probing tongue slipped inside me. The loud sucking sounds she made filled my ears as she cupped my quivering buttocks and slipped her thumb inside my anus.

By then I was squeezing and rolling my nipples between my fingers and found myself arching my back off the bed, the orgasm seizing every nerve and sending my soul into space before it shattered into millions of tiny shards that gently floated back down to earth.

It was then I heard the low, hissing sounds escaping my open mouth and I couldn't help but laugh at that, the low giggles escaping Naseem's lovely mouth between long, teasing licks to my juicy pussy sounding so sexy.

After a few moments she moved her now naked body over mine, her nipples tracing lines of electricity on my thighs and belly until our hard-tipped breasts rubbed against each other, our mouths melting into a deep, probing kiss, our tongues a pair of mating snakes. I relished the taste of my pussy mixed with her sweet breath as we rolled on the bed, my fingers finding their way between her legs as I moved my lips down to her nipples and sucked away. The low moans escaping her mouth, the wet, rolling sensation of her lips between my fingers as I reached around to cup her gorgeous, ivory bottom, bringing us even closer in our embrace was absolute heaven.

Just as I felt the first shivers of her orgasm course through her body I moved down between her legs and feasted away, her pussy lips feeling and tasting so good in my mouth.

She treated me to the twin pleasures of having my pussy and anus licked and probed and when I returned the favour, my tongue filling that wet, tiny opening as my thumb slipped inside her pliant back door, I felt her heave and shudder.

Her low moans got even louder as she rubbed and massaged my back while clamping her thighs around my head. When her pelvis quivered and heaved against my face a loud moan escaped her lovely mouth, her body heaving and shuddering until she collapsed on the bed, her silken thighs still wrapped around my head, her tiny feet resting on my back.

We lay on the bed under the sheets, our bodies entwined around each other while sharing a cool glass of wine and trading soft, tender kisses, at times passing the wine between our mouths, our tongues wrestling in a slow, gentle manner until we went to sleep.

The next morning I woke up alone, the scent of Naseem's body still lingering under the sheets, a single red rose on the other pillow, a familiar-looking delicate gold chain threaded around the stem. I didn't feel sad or abandoned, recalling what she said about being not being into "long-term commitments" and knew if I pursued her things would only get awkward.

Instead, I wrapped the little gold chain around my ankle (it fitted perfectly) admiring the way it looked while pointing my toes and raising my leg, letting the shadows play on the definitions of my thigh and calf.

Then, I held the rose close to my face, took a deep breath, my other hand caressing my body, and slowly recalled the sweet memory of our night together, knowing I would cherish it for the rest of my life.

Meeting Jane
by January James

I am a thirty-four year old woman with an unusual fetish that I never thought I'd get to experience until I met Jane. I have a serious fascination with pregnant women. To me, they are always beautiful and sexy. I'm the Suicide Girl type, with tattoos, a stud above my lip and a ring in the lower one. With short dark hair, multiple earrings and big tits and sultry grey eyes, I can turn a few heads with my tough girl image but I didn't even have the courage to be myself, until Jane.

When a woman is expecting, something changes in the way she walks, in the way she holds her place in the universe, and I fall completely in love. I can't walk by a pregnant woman without asking to touch her belly. They have no idea how deeply that thrill affects me. Browsing around the Internet, I know I'm not a freak, or alone. There are many, male and female, who love getting hot and bothered over the miracle of pregnancy. But most of us can only indulge in front of the computer or TV and I had resigned myself to this fate until Jane came into my life.

We met at a coffee shop one morning when I popped in for my usual caffeine hit and some stimulating conversation with other aspiring writers and artists. Jane was the new girl behind the counter with the sunny smile that didn't quite dispel the boredom in her beautiful brown eyes.

"It helps if you think about something else," I offered when she handed me my mocha soy latte and my change.

She smiled. "I see you've been here before."

Returning her smile, I held out my hand. "I'm Aurora and yes, I know exactly what you're going through. I had writing to keep me company so I was always making up stories in my head."

"I'm Jane. I dabble with writing here and there but I never thought I could make a living at it."

"Yeah you can. Hey, I live in the little apartment right around the corner. Why don't you stop by sometime and I'll show you some of my works."

Jane came by the next day and sort of never left. It didn't take long for her to confide that she was having problems with her boyfriend and how much she hated living at her parents' house.

"Well you can crash here as long as you need to," I offered. I'd also been down that road before and knew how tough it was.

Jane shook her head. "I don't think I can impose like that and besides, I'm pregnant. I think that's a little more than you can handle."

In all honesty, it never entered my mind that I could get lucky with Jane. I saw where she needed a friend and I was willing to help. But as our relationship, and her stomach grew, I fantasized about having her.

Jane was a beautiful woman, with or without her baby bump. She had long, dark brown hair, Mediterranean skin and features, legs for days and big, natural tits. As she progressed in her pregnancy, she blossomed from beautiful into breathtaking.

I managed to hold my feelings in check, only unleashing my desires alone at night in the safety of my makeshift studio bedroom. Jane was going back and forth between facing motherhood alone and getting back with her boyfriend.

"We didn't want a baby right now and it's driving us both crazy," she explained after one of their fights, after which she came crying to me. Brad's really a good guy and he loves me. This is just a rough time for us right now. But I know we'll manage to work things out."

I handed her a cup of herbal tea. "Still, you shouldn't fight so much, it's not good for the baby." Having Jane in my life made me more caring, took the edge off my tough girl attitude. Jane required more than she was able to give and it felt good to think of someone other than myself.

A vision of her floated into my mind as I lay spread-eagled and naked in bed later that night. Jane naked was the most awe inspiring sight I'd ever seen.

Her breasts were so ripe; I itched to touch them and actually had to clench my naughty fingers into fists to keep from grabbing her as she lounged naked on my bed, rubbing herself with cocoa butter.

She'd waved away my apologies the first time I'd walked in on her naked on my way to the one bathroom.

"Please, we're all girls here. I won't be able to see my own feet in a few months, who knows what I may need you to do for me."

After that, I made a point of going into the bathroom right after she'd had her bath, when the warmth of her skin still lingered in the air. I inhaled her coconut shampoo, the hint of Ivory soap. I touched my breasts, imagining they were hers, hanging like ripe, oversized mangoes from my gamma's Florida garden.

I used to watch the mangoes every day when I spent my summers with her. I wanted to pick them right away but I knew if I left them a little longer, they would get bigger and juicier and soon, my patience would be rewarded with sweet, sticky yellow juice running down my hands as I bit into the succulent fruit.

I'd imagined what Jane's breasts would be like in three months when she entered her last trimester. They'd be all engorged with milk, like beautiful giant penises primed for ejaculation.

I wanted them to come on me; I wanted her milk mingling with my juices in my pussy. I wanted to taste it, her life force flowing from her body into my open, hungry mouth. I didn't realise I was pulling on my own nipples until I accidentally pinched one a little too hard. My pussy was an aching, twitching hole insistent on being filled. I felt an intense heat and an overwhelming need that had been building for months.

I'd written many stories about running my tongue against the slickness of a pussy preparing to be a gateway into the world. An expecting pussy holds so much power, so much divine orchestration. In my dreams it's always a transcendental experience.

I hadn't tasted anyone other than myself in a long time. I wanted to be fucked with something big and silicone with Jane attached to it. I parted my cunt with fingers sporting short nails with black polish. I was so wet it dripped down to the crack of my ass.

I flipped over onto all fours and pushed my shoulders and tits into the bed. I slid my breasts against the coarse afghan quilt I'd bought from a pregnant vendor five years earlier on a trip to Morocco.

I'd gone back to my hotel, wrapped myself in it and masturbated as I imagined her naked, her beautiful brown

191

body glistening under mine as I enjoyed her exotic cunt.

I stuck my ass in the air and placed my hands underneath me. I cupped my pussy then slipped my middle finger inside and caressed my wet lips. I eased the finger in then thumbed my swollen clit; pressing into it so hard I shuddered. I played with my pussy until my hand is frothy and my hips are bucking like a video vixen intent on hip hop glory.

I replaced the wet hand with the dry one, flung the wet one over my hip, and tunneled my middle finger into my taut behind.

I whispered Jane's name, my voice a soft litany of confessions of all the things I wanted to do to her and with her. I pushed another finger into my pussy, groaned, and pushed in a third. It felt so good. My confessions soon turned into a prayer of sorts, of what I hoped would be until finally, conversation became too distracting and I bit down on my bottom lip. There's no sound except for the wet, slushy music of finger fucking until I erupted in a groan that started out as a wail, then combined with my orgasm for a headlong rush through my entire body.

As the weeks slipped by, the coffee house started taking its toll on Jane. Her manager allowed me to take over her shifts whenever she was too beat to make it in. Whenever she was able to go in, she came home half dead but loaded with tips.

"I think most of the customers feel sorry for me at this point," she said after flopping down on the bed.

I'd help her out of her clothes and into a warm shower. She couldn't get up out of the tub so easily any more. I sat on the toilet and asked her about her shift to keep her from falling asleep under the dribble of hard water my landlord kept reminding me I was lucky to have. Afterwards, I rubbed coco butter all over her beautiful body and we'd sip green tea and munch on dark chocolate brownies while she read me her poetry.

"You really should join Spoken Word at the coffee shop," I told her one night as we lounged on the couch. "Your poems speak to so much of what women are facing these days."

Her self-deprecating laugh touched me. "You mean like how we keep bringing children into our toxic little worlds and expect them to be well adjusted human beings?"

"Then why don't you just leave Brad and make a life with someone else?"

She shook her head. "It's more complicated than that. I bring my own set of demons to our relationship. He wants to marry me, you know? His family is religious and they don't want a bastard. But I don't want him marrying me just because he knocked me up, I want him to do it because he loves me."

The baby kicked and we both placed our hands on her stomach.

"This is so amazing," she said breathlessly. "I still can't believe there's a life growing inside me."

"Do you think Brad loves you?" I asked.

Jane popped the last piece of brownie in her mouth and chewed slowly before answering. "My mother doesn't think I'm loveable. I've never allowed myself to believe it even though he tells me all the time."

I reached up and caressed the side of her face, smoothing her silky hair behind her ear. "In the time I've know you, I think you are exceptional in so many ways, Jane Bolin."

We stared at each other while my heart beat erratically in my chest.

"Have you ever been in love?" Jane asked.

I lowered my eyes. "I thought I was in love. Paul and I grew up together. Our families are both what you would call high society and my parents thought he was perfect for me. We were two months from walking down the aisle before I finally found the courage to call it off."

"It's hard to escape your parents expectations, good or bad," Jane surmised.

I nodded. "I had to find how I felt about myself more than how I felt about Paul. I didn't know who I was so I walked away from what was expected of me to find out."

Jane smiled. "And some kind soul took you in and now you're returning the favour."

"I see a lot of myself in you," I told her quietly.

"And have you found yourself?" she asked.

"I think I've always known, it was just a matter of accepting."

"So what were you hiding?"

"How much I wanted to hold someone soft and female, how being with a woman makes so much sense since we're wired in the same way. But maybe it's just a fantasy and not something I really want."

"But you're lonely, I can see it in your eyes," Jane observed. "So, shouldn't you at least find out?"

I wiped at unexpected tears. "I guess. I've buried myself in my work, maybe because I don't have the courage to actually put my heart out there for another woman to trample."

Jane reached out and took my hand. "I know what it feels like to be kicked in the teeth by love." She caressed my palm with her thumb. "Maybe you can start with just giving your body, just enjoy being with a woman without stressing about finding someone to spend the rest of your life with." She leaned in and kissed my cheek.

I inhaled her scent. "Have you done this before, been

with a woman?" I asked.

"I don't see people in terms of gender but in the kinds of connections I share with them," she explained.

"That must complicate things with Brad."

"Do you want to talk about Brad or do you want to fuck me?" she asked.

"I want to fuck you," I said simply but no four words had ever sounded so poetic.

Jane leaned in and kissed my cheek softly, her lips barely a whisper on my overheated skin. She trailed down, her chocolate breath a mere caress until she reached my lips. The air caught in my lungs as her mouth descended and I held on to every millisecond until her softness exploded around me.

Her tongue traced the contours of my lips before delving into the warmth of my mouth. She took her time, allowing me to get used to the texture of her tongue, the feel of it exploring, tasting, and taking. My hands went out and I clung to her as I tried to match her fervour. Jane knew how a woman liked to be kissed, and touched, I soon learned as her hands travelled down to my breasts.

I don't remember when our clothes came off. That mundane memory has been blocked to make room for the feel of her skin against my hand, her heartbeat, slow and steady as we gazed at each other around the wonderment of what we shared.

She sprawled out on the sofa. "I'm all yours," she said opening her legs and her arms.

I moved between them and kissed her until she begged me to go lower. I ran my tongue down the centre of her torso, down to her beautiful stomach bypassing the succulent milk-filled mounds. I was afraid of coming as soon as my mouth latched onto one big, glorious nipple. I felt the baby kick against my touch making my pussy

195

twitch to the point of pain.

I felt the heat from her pussy, calling me, luring me to the slickness between her thighs but I managed to resist by focusing on her heavy breasts. I touched them reverently, my fingers trembling against the taut skin.

Jane sighed and bolstered the feeling that I was doing something right, I took her right nipple into my mouth. I suckled her like an infant, I couldn't help it. I wanted to lie in her arms and have those massive tits hang over me. I wanted to drown in their taste and smell, in the life sustaining nectar that seemed so close. I knew if I suckled long enough and was patient, just like my grandmother's mangoes, I'd be rewarded with the best fruit Mother Nature could make.

I slid down her body and finally heeded the calls of her pussy. I explored hers carefully, despite her insistence that I was driving her out of her mind. Her wiggling hips didn't help matters either. This was the first time I'd beheld the beauty of the pussy, it was like a Georgia O'Keefe painting, and I was spellbound. I wanted to worship at the altar of her cunt. She was wet and pleasantly musky and the feel of her against my tongue, all slick and pouting, was surreal.

She screamed as I ate her, used my fingers to stroke her little nubbin of hard flesh. She creamed easily and came quickly, releasing a warm gush of pussy juice that ran down my chin. I looked up at her and smiled. Her face was dreamy but she managed to sit up.

"Now let me show you what it feels like to be on the receiving end," she offered.

"No, there'll be time for that later, there's something else that I've always wanted to try."

Jane smiled curiously. "I'm game for anything."

I squatted over her, opened my pussy lips, and started

rubbing my clit over her stomach. I was mindful that I had to be gentle but it took very little pressure on her before I came. I grabbed the back of the sofa and cried out as a glorious flush of pleasure washed over me.

We moved to the bedroom where Jane showed me the joys of receiving. Over the next few months, we did use a strap-on and I finally tasted Jane's milk, filling my mouth and my pussy. It was the best come, my addiction, and I wondered how I would live without it.

I felt it when she was ready to leave, but I was too afraid to say anything. I guess she was too, because she chose a unique way to say goodbye, at the place where we'd first met.

A single spotlight highlighted her onstage. Jane was truly breathtaking; her skin glowed from being pregnant and nervous about her first time pouring out her feelings to a room full of strangers. She sought my eyes in the crowd. I gave her the thumbs up. I'd assured her numerous times that her work was good and as she delved into her first poem the audience soon confirmed it. Their applause made it a little easier for her to move on to the next.

After the last one we'd rehearsed, Jane surprised me with a dedication.

"I want you to know how special you are to me," she began looking right at me.

As each line flowed, I realised she was breaking up with me. It was a goodbye poem, one in which she told me how I'd saved her life, how she would always love me, but she wanted to raise her baby with Brad.

I don't remember who started first, but soon we were both crying. I felt like my heart was breaking, but it wasn't because she was leaving me. I wanted her to be with Brad. I knew how much she loved him.

My heart broke for the woman I used to be, the one who'd spent her entire life trying to please her parents. Jane was the best way for me to ease into the lesbian lifestyle. I'd known my heart was safe with her because we'd shared so much of the same issues. And the sex was the most incredible experience of my life.

When I got home Jane was gone and I was glad. I wouldn't have been able to say goodbye to her. She left a note reiterating what she said at the club. Her presence still lingered everywhere in the small apartment.

I curled up in my bed, pressing my face into the pillow she'd slept on for seven months. It smelled of cocoa butter and Ivory soap, coconut shampoo and desire, our desire. I hugged it to me like a lover and fell asleep with Jane's voice in my head and the essence of her wrapped all around me.

The next morning I faced life after Jane. It hurt not having her at my poor excuse for a dining table, with the morning sun streaming through her hair as she ploughed through a stack of pancakes. I missed the companionable silence as we wrote or read side by side during the day and the nights we spent out on the strip of balcony talking about our futures.

But as the days slipped by, I learned to live without her memory as my constant companion. About a month later, I got an e-mail stating she'd given birth to a baby girl and she and Brad were getting married. She invited me to the wedding and of course I plan to attend. Hopefully we can continue to be great friends, though I hold no illusions about us ever getting together again. My time with Jane was a gift, not a relationship. She was brought into my life at a time when I needed the courage to fully embrace who I am. I'll always be grateful for that.

Some people believe fantasies should remain as such, that it's never as good as you've imagined them to be. I have to say that indulging in my fetish for pregnant women went beyond anything I could've dreamt up. It was truly incredible and the most amazing way to introduce me to the many joys of being with another woman. I have Jane to thank for that.